'I'm not a sadist. Whatever you think, I don't like seeing people suffer.'

'Not even me?' Jake persisted grimly, and Abby dragged her eyes away from his to assume a contemplation of the coverlet.

'Not even you,' she conceded, and then gasped in surprise when his hands closed over hers.

'Don't do that,' he said, causing her startled gaze to seek his. 'I'm not your responsibility. If I choose to go to hell my own way, then you don't have to get involved.'

'But I am involved,' said Abby.

INDISCRETION

BY

ANNE MATHER

MILLS & BOON LIMITED
ETON HOUSE   18-24 PARADISE ROAD
RICHMOND   SURREY   TW9 1SR

*First published in Great Britain 1990
by Mills & Boon Limited*

© Anne Mather 1990

*Australian copyright 1990
Philippine copyright 1990
This edition 1990*

ISBN 0 263 76773 6

*Set in Times Roman 10 on 11 pt.
01-9008-59223 C*

Made and printed in Great Britain

CHAPTER ONE

FROM the deck of the inter-island ferry, Laguna Cay looked green and exotic—and frustratingly familiar. Frustratingly so, because Abby had hoped that her memories might have exaggerated its warmth, and light, and colour; but, of course, they hadn't. If anything, it looked even more lush and tropical now than she remembered it, its sun-drenched harbour a glowing introduction to forty square miles of verdant paradise.

But paradise of a geographical sort only, she mentally corrected herself, her hands tightening involuntarily on the ship's rail. From her own point of view, it had proved to be anything but paradisaical, and she had left Laguna Cay vowing never to come back.

Not that she had had much choice in the matter, she reflected, with reluctant honesty. To be absolutely factual, she had been escorted off the island, and tears had blinded her last glimpses of Sandbar through the windows of Jake's executive jet. But she had sworn never to come back, even if, at that time, she had had no idea that Jake might get custody of Dominic.

Abby took a deep breath and released her fingers from the rail, rubbing her sticky palms down the seams of her denim skirt. She had to calm down, she told herself, aware that she was already allowing her nerves to get the better of her. She wasn't coming here unannounced. Julie had invited her. There was no point in getting strung up about the situation when she didn't even know all the facts.

Her palms clung to the thin denim, briefly drawing the hem higher up her thigh, and as she hurried to

smooth it down again Abby realised her actions were
being monitored by a group of seamen lounging in the
stern. Ordinarily, she would have ignored their observation. Goodness knew, she was used to being stared at
by all sectors of the population, including those who got
their kicks from leering at any good-looking woman. But
today, with her emotions so close to the surface, she was
in no mood to humour anyone, and, subjecting the men
to a cold-eyed stare, she determinedly turned her back.

But the reasons for their attention were not so easy
to dismiss. Looking down, she viewed what she was
wearing through their eyes, and found it wanting. The
slim-fitting denim skirt, whose hem settled a bare inch
above her knee, had seemed a fairly modest compromise
that morning, back in her hotel room in Nassau. Looking
though her window, she had seen women in much shorter
skirts, and scanty shorts, so that her outfit of a dark
blue silk vest and the denim skirt had looked almost
conservative. The trouble was, because she was five feet
ten inches tall, men tended to look at her legs first, and
she found herself wishing desperately that she had worn
trousers.

But it was so hot, and humid. The Bahamas in June
was not her most favourite place to be, and the idea of
again putting on the cotton trousers she had worn on
the flight from London had not been appealing. Which
meant that her choice was limited to the shorts she had
brought to wear at Sandbar, or one of two skirts and
three summer dresses, the hems of which were all cropped
this season.

Putting up her hand, she lifted the weight of her hair
away from her neck, this time happily unconscious of
other eyes appraising the way the movement outlined
the uplifted curve of her breasts against the thin fabric
of the vest. The lacy bra, that cupped the deliciously
generous flesh, barely concealed its delicate burden, and
the captain of the ferry boat rolled his eyes expressively

at Abby's innocent exposure. He couldn't help wondering why the pretty lady was coming back to the island. It was common knowledge why she had left, after all. It had to be something to do with Mr Lowell. But, remembering how the Boss Man had thrown her out, he didn't think *he* could know anything about her return. Unless, after what had happened...

But they were approaching the quay, and the captain's speculations had to be cut short as all his attention was regrettably required to bring the ferry into harbour. The inter-island steamer was the only public means of access to Laguna Cay, the coral reef that surrounded the island successfully preventing any unscheduled arrivals. In any case, there were no hotels on the island, and no tourists were allowed. Anyone disembarking there had to produce evidence that they were legitimate visitors. And, as most of Mr Lowell's guests were flown in personally, it was seldom that Captain Rodrigues delivered anything more than supplies.

The small harbour was thronged with fishing boats, however. The inhabitants of the island mostly made their living from the sea. Fish caught off Laguna Cay, and the nearby Abacos Islands, was sold in Nassau and Grand Bahama, and the fishermen and their families lived in relative comfort. The fertile soil of the island and the consistently warm weather also enabled them to practise a certain amount of self-sufficiency, and the good health of its people was a measure of Laguna Cay's success.

Of course, it had to be said that before Jake Lowell bought the island fifteen years ago things were not as they were today. The indigenous population had been quite content to eke out a living from day to day, and it took Jake several years to persuade them to reorganise themselves. But Jake was very good at persuading people to do things, reflected Abby bitterly, remembering only too well how he had convinced the judge to let *him* bring up *her* son. The fact that Dominic was his son, too, was immaterial. She was the child's mother. She should have been granted that right.

Black hands reached for the ropes as the ferry nudged the stone quay, and Abby flexed her long fingers as she prepared to disembark. She had one suitcase—optimistic perhaps, but she couldn't travel without a change of clothes, could she?—and a soft leather holdall, that contained her travel documents and more personal items. The matching taupe leather jacket she had needed in London was tucked casually through the straps of the holdall, and she slung the holdall over her shoulder as she waited for the ropes to be moored.

'Mr Lowell is expecting you, is he not?'

The liquid tones of Captain Rodrigues momentarily diverted her from her anxious inspection of the quay, and Abby turned to look at him with what she hoped was a confident smile. 'I am expected, yes,' she conceded, almost but not quite answering his question. 'Thank you for a very pleasant journey. I enjoyed it.'

Captain Rodrigues returned her smile, his dark face, with its thin waxed moustache, mirroring his admiration. 'I am happy to have been of service,' he assured her smoothly. 'Perhaps we can be of service again, when you return to New Providence.'

'Perhaps you can.' Abby gave a nervous shrug, before returning her attention to the throng of dark faces gathering to watch the ferry disembark. But she doubted it. No matter how ill Jake might be, she couldn't imagine him letting her take Dominic on the inter-island ferry.

The ribbed gangways were being run out, and with a brief gesture of farewell to the captain Abby moved forward. Not that there was any rush to disembark. Apart from herself, there was only one other passenger on the ferry, and as he had friends among the crew he was in no hurry to get off the ship.

As she negotiated the slope down to the quay, Abby let her eyes wander beyond the sea of curious faces to the rows of pink-washed dwellings, stepping up the wooded hillside behind the harbour. Coral roofs climbed, one upon the other, interspersed here and there with wrought-iron balconies and clinging vines. The heat was more palpable here, caught in the bowl of the surrounding cliffs, and without the breeze that came off the water Abby could feel beads of sweat breaking out all over her.

And where was Julie? she fretted worriedly, as she took her first steps on the island for six years. Jake's sister had promised she would be here to meet her. Surely she was not going to let her down? Not after she had come all this way.

She saw the dark-skinned harbour master making his way towards her, and her heart sank. Like Captain Rodrigues, and probably everybody else, she reflected resignedly, he must know she had left the island rather precipitately. The last thing she wanted to have to do was explain herself to him. But if Julie didn't arrive soon, what alternative was she going to have?

And then, as she was turning to thank the member of the crew who had hefted her suitcase to the quay, she heard the welcome roar of a car's engine. Swinging round, she was in time to see the open-topped Jeep as it careered down the final few yards of the hill, and then skidded through the rapidly parting crowds to brake to a halt beside her.

The young woman who got out of the Jeep was unmistakably Jake's sister. She had the same dark hair and olive-tinted skin, the same lean build, the same economy of movement. But there the resemblance ended. For, where Jake was tall, Julie was of only average height, and the angular features which looked so good on her brother were infinitely less attractive in a feminine mould. Yet, for all that, Julie was very attractive, not least because she had a warm-hearted, vibrant personality. And she and her husband, David Spannier, had always been good friends of Abby's, albeit that that friendship had been left pending when Abby had returned to London.

'Abby!' she exclaimed now, covering the space between them in a few short strides, and unhesitatingly throwing her arms about her. 'Oh, Abby, it's so good to see you! And I had to be late. Isn't that typical?'

Abby returned the hug with interest, her relief at seeing Jake's sister again almost overwhelming her. It had been such a long journey, fraught with fears and anxieties, and doubts about its advisability. But no longer. Julie's welcome convinced her that she had done the right thing in responding to her invitation, and the prospect of seeing Dominic again was now an imminent reality.

'It's good to see you again, Julie,' she endorsed, as the other girl drew back to look at her. 'I was half afraid you weren't going to make it, and I wasn't looking forward to explaining my reasons for being here to Andy Joseph.'

'Oh, Andy takes himself too seriously,' declared Julie, as, having assured himself that Abby was indeed expected, the harbour master turned back to his office. 'Anyway, that's not important now. I'm here. So let me look at you. Gosh, you haven't changed at all, do you know that? I'd forgotten how beautiful you really are. David would flip his lid to see you!'

Abby pulled a wry face. 'I doubt it,' she averred drily, knowing how close the bond was between Julie and her husband. 'How is David, anyway? And Ruth and Penny.'

'They're OK.' Julie spoke carelessly. 'Dave's working as hard as ever, and the other two are in school now. Penny is in Miami, and Ruth at boarding school in Boston. She's twelve now, you know. And Penny's almost ten.'

'Really!' Abby was astounded. 'I still picture them as—well, as I last saw them.'

'Yes, I know. I guess we all do the same.' Julie grimaced. 'Although, in your case, we weren't far wrong.' She bent to pick up Abby's suitcase, and gestured towards the Jeep. 'Come on, let's go. We're wasting time standing chatting here. I guess you're dying to see Dominic, aren't you? I know I would be in your position.'

Abby hefted her own bag, and climbed into the front of the Jeep beside Julie. Her longer legs made riding in the confines of the Jeep less comfortable than it was for Jake's sister, but at least there was no man around to gape at her uncovered thighs, she thought, relaxing a little. It was a relief, too, to get away from the curious eyes surrounding her. If she had wanted her arrival to be more public, she doubted she could have made it so.

But once the adaptable little vehicle had turned, and was labouring gallantly up the winding track out of the little port of Laguna Cay, Abby was able to anticipate her meeting with her son with real excitement. It was nine months since she had seen him, the month he should have spent with her at Christmas cancelled because Jake had informed her, through his solicitors, that Dominic had a cold, and was unfit to travel to a chilly climate. Abby had been disappointed, of course, but as it happened she had been offered an assignment in India, and, although she had been loath to leave London in case Jake should change his mind, Marcia had persuaded her that she'd be wasting her time.

'So,' she said now, turning to Julie, 'how is he?'

'Dominic?' Julie shrugged. 'He's fine.'

'I meant Jake,' said Abby evenly, despising the sudden twist she felt at even saying his name. 'You said—you said he'd collapsed and been taken to hospital. How—serious is it?'

Julie's tongue circled her lips, and Abby got the distinct impression that the other girl was anxious now. But why? What had gone wrong? A thought struck her. Surely this hadn't all been a ruse of Julie's, to get her to come out here.

'He did collapse, didn't he?' she hastened now, before Julie could reply. 'This isn't just——'

'No, he collapsed all right.' Julie glanced her way, her features somewhat strained. 'They think—they think it was—overwork, stress, call it what you like. Ever since— well, ever since he married Eve, he's been working himself to death. But, he wouldn't listen to anyone, of course. You know what Jake is like.'

Did she? Abby breathed a sigh. 'But when you phoned, you said—Eve—was gone.' It hurt to say her name, too. It hurt to think that Jake had married someone else only weeks after their son was born.

'Oh, yes.' Julie spoke more confidently now. 'I told you. That was over ages ago. That was why I rang you. With Jake in hospital, and only the servants here to care for him, Dominic needed his mother.'

Abby took a breath, turning to stare out at the passing scenery. Just for a moment, the realisation that she would be seeing her son again in less than fifteen minutes caught the back of her throat. Nine months was too long. She hoped he hadn't forgotten her.

Below them now, the lace-edged beaches of Laguna Cay curved below the swell of the cliffs. The road at this point followed the contours of the bluff, only winding down again when they reached Heron's Point, and the track down to Sandbar. The road itself wound through a tangle of vegetation, with hedges of scarlet hibiscus giving the air a subtle fragrance.

'I sometimes wonder why Jake ever married her.' Julie's voice drew Abby unwillingly back to the reasons for her visit. 'I don't think he loved her. He certainly never gave that impression.'

'Didn't he?' Abby was obliged to make some response, so she made it. But she knew why Jake had married Eve. Or, at least, she thought she did. With a wife to endorse his paternity, it had been so much easier to convince a judge of his stability, and Abby's lack of it. And with boundless wealth besides, how could he have failed?

'Still,' she said now, reluctantly forced to face the present situation, 'you didn't tell me how he is. How long do you expect him to remain in hospital? Will he need nursing treatment when he gets home?'

The pregnant silence that followed tore Abby's nerves to shreds. For a few ominous moments all she could hear was the low thunder of the surf as they rounded the point, and the accelerating pulse of her own heartbeat. For several seconds Julie said nothing, nothing at all; but by the time she did summon up the courage to meet Abby's disbelieving eyes, Abby knew exactly what she was going to say.

'He's not in hospital, is he?' she asked, in a small cold voice. And then, with anguish, 'Oh, Julie, how *could* you?'

'Now, don't go getting upset——'

'Why not? Does he know I'm here?'

'No, but—oh, Abby, it's not the way you think.' Julie kept her eyes on the road with an effort, her fingers clasping and unclasping around the wheel. 'He—he *was* in hospital. Until yesterday afternoon, actually. And there was no way I was going to ring you at the hotel in Nassau and tell you not to come. He *should* still be in hospital. Honestly, it's the truth.'

The sweaty feeling Abby had had down at the quayside was magnified now, a hundredfold. Dear God, she thought sickly, and she had been anticipating seeing Dominic again with such enthusiasm. Instead of which, she was going to see Jake, and the way he would feel about her coming here she'd be lucky if she even got to see her son!

'Look, you're jumping to all the wrong conclusions,' said Julie frustratedly, aware of Abby's draining colour and the perspiration beading her upper lip. 'Calm down, can't you?'

'Are you serious?' Abby moved her head from side to side as the full implications of the bombshell Jake's sister had exploded washed over her. 'Julie, I came here because I thought Dominic needed me. But if his father's home from hospital——'

'So what?' Julie obviously wished she were doing anything other than driving a vehicle at that moment, and Abby winced as the wheels of the Jeep swept dangerously near the edge of the cliff. 'You're his mother, Abby. Since Eve went away, he hasn't even had an apology for one. Do you want your son to be brought up by his nanny? Do you want him to forget that he ever had a mother?'

'Of course not.' Abby was indignant. 'I never wanted that, and you know it.'

'So what am I saying?'

'Yes, but——' Abby gnawed anxiously at her bottom lip. 'Jake will never let me stay here.'

'I doubt if he'll have much choice, at the moment,' retorted Julie fiercely. 'You don't seem to understand, Abby. Jake is in no state to make ultimatums. And don't forget, now that Eve isn't here any more the legal situation may not be as black and white as it once was.'

'What do you mean?' Abby stared at her.

Julie shrugged, looking a little discomfited now. Jake was her brother, after all, and Abby guessed she hadn't enjoyed deceiving him. But nevertheless her words had to mean something, and after a moment Abby thought she began to understand. As her colour returned to bring a hectic flush to her cheeks she began to think for herself, and the spark of hope that had been kindled when Julie first got in touch with her in England flared anew. Could Eve's departure have anything to do with Jake's reasons for not allowing her son to come to England for Christmas? she wondered. Had Dominic's cold—if, indeed, he had had one—merely been a convenient excuse to avoid that revelation? For without a doubt Dominic would have told her that his stepmother was no longer living at Sandbar, and with that ammunition Abby might have risked another offensive.

But then something else Julie had said occurred to her, and, putting aside her own ambitions for the moment, she said, 'Why did you say Jake was in no state to make ultimatums? If he was capable of discharging himself from the hospital——'

'In Miami, yes,' agreed Julie, nodding, as the Jeep bucketed over the ridge and then began the tortuous descent towards Oleander Bay. 'But I also said he should still be in the hospital. He should. He needs rest and relaxation, but since he came home he's hardly been off the phone. He's a fool, because he can't afford to take chances. If he's not careful, he's going to have a really serious heart attack.'

Abby, whose eyes had been drawn to the long sweep of coral sand that curved round the bay, now turned sharply to the other woman. 'What did you say?' she gasped. 'I thought you told me he'd collapsed from stress, and overwork!' Her own heart palpitated wildly as she stared at her companion. 'Julie, are you saying he had a heart attack? My God! Is he all right?'

She didn't know why she was so agitated, but she was, and Julie glanced at her with troubled eyes. 'I—the doctors said it—could have been a mild coronary,' she admitted reluctantly. 'Apparently people have them all the time.'

'Is there such a thing?' Abby was barely convinced. 'A *mild* coronary! Julie, that sounds like a contradiction in terms.'

'Well, I don't know, do I?' Julie herself sounded a little upset now. 'All I know is, he was unconscious when they took him to the hospital, and when we went to see him, they had him in the ICU.'

'Which was when?'

'Five—six days ago. You know when I rang you.'

'Yes, but you didn't say Jake had had a heart attack!'

'I didn't know, did I? I phoned you before there was any real news. I thought you'd want to know.'

'Yes.' Abby tried to calm down. 'Yes, I did.' It wasn't Julie's fault, after all. It wasn't Julie's fault that Jake was crazy enough to take unnecessary risks with his health. It wasn't Julie's fault that Abby suddenly felt so responsible. And it was nothing to do with her, either. It was almost six years since she and Jake had met, face to face. And it was ridiculous now for her to feel so anxious. Jake would not thank her for it. She had no illusions about that.

'Anyway, if he was in danger of having a relapse they wouldn't have let him come home, would they?' Julie argued now, evidently needing some reassurance herself. But Abby couldn't give it.

'Could they stop him?' she asked laconically, and Julie's look of doubt almost exactly matched her own.

'Well—you'll just have to see he takes it easy for the next couple of weeks,' Julie declared eventually, and Abby caught her breath at the blatant allegation.

'*Me?*'

'Well, I can't stay, can I?' Julie stated. 'Dave's already been on the phone a couple of times, asking when I'm coming back. But so long as Jake was in hospital I knew I couldn't leave Dominic.'

'So you phoned me.' Abby was beginning to wonder if coming here had been such a good idea, after all. 'Julie, I have a job to do, too. True, I've got a week's leave coming to me, but after that I'm expected back. It's the autumn collections in September, and there are dozens of photographic sessions before then.'

Julie took a deep breath. 'I thought you were eager to spend some time with Dominic.'

'I am.' Abby sighed. 'But I hoped you'd let me take him back with me.'

'To England?'

'Where else?'

'But his home's here.'

'Only so long as he lives with Jake,' said Abby flatly, realising that for all her understanding Julie was still Jake's sister first and her friend second. 'Do you think Jake will let me do that? Bearing in mind what you said about his wife.'

'His ex-wife. They're divorced,' said Julie shortly, using the correction as a diversion. 'But—no. I don't suppose Jake will want you to take his son back to England. That's something the two of you have to work out. You—you and Jake together.'

His son! Abby's lips tightened, as she turned her attention back to the view. The Lowells were always going to regard Dominic as *Jake's* son. The fact that she had carried him around in her body for nine months and then given painful birth to him didn't seem to register. She *was* his mother. But her contribution was overlooked.

The road was levelling out now, and on their left clusters of feathery palm trees edged the shore. The breeze was welcome, too, sweeping in off the water, whose colours ranged from deepest blue to palest green. In the shallows, gulls and herons waded, ducking their heads in search of food, and further along there would be land crabs, and shallow pools where grey snapper could be caught by the least experienced of fishermen.

Abby didn't want to remember, but as they grew nearer to Jake's home she couldn't help it. After all, she and Jake used to walk here, morning and night, dipping into rock pools and paddling in the creaming surf. It was Jake who had taught her to snorkel, and to scuba dive, taking her out to the reef and showing her all the many dozens of exotic species of fish that swam in and out of the living coral. He had even taken her big game fishing, although the idea of capturing one of the huge marlin or tuna that inhabited the deeper waters just for the thrill of boasting about it later had not been to her taste.

Turning her head away from memories that were still too disturbing to her peace of mind, Abby saw the rolling dunes of the golf course that Jake had had landscaped, chiefly for the benefit of his guests. Jake himself didn't play—or at least he hadn't, when she'd left the island, she amended silently—but Sandbar catered to all tastes and all forms of relaxation. There was a huge swimming-pool, she remembered, and tennis-courts, not to mention a squash court and gymnasium, with an adjoining sauna facility.

Jake should have been fit, Abby reflected now, her nerves prickling again in anticipation of seeing him once more. The trouble was, he had always spent too much time making money to have any time to spend it. Even in the early days of their relationship, the telephone had made him too accessible, and the leisure empire he had built from the six run-down hotels his father had left him had usually had first call on his attention.

She could see Sandbar now. The rambling two-storeyed dwelling that Jake had built with his first million sprawled on a grassy knoll overlooking the languid waters of Oleander Bay. No one knew who had first named the graceful indentation in the coastline, but the reasons why it had been chosen were fairly evident. Oleanders in every shade of pink and red and white grew in wild profusion everywhere, their leathery leaves soaking up the moisture and giving off their own distinctive perfume.

'You wouldn't—I mean, you won't say anything to upset him, will you?'

Julie was evidently nervous too, and Abby could see the way her knuckles showed white where she was gripping the steering-wheel. She supposed it had been easy for Julie to convince herself she was doing the right thing when an actual confrontation between her brother and the mother of his child had not been imminent. No doubt she had expected that Abby would be prepared to stay at Sandbar for a while, giving her plenty of time to break the news gently. But now the situation had changed, and Abby suspected she was half regretting her impulsiveness. After all, Jake had discharged himself from hospital, long before he should, and Abby was talking about taking Dominic back to England.

'Don't worry,' Abby told her reassuringly, twisting the strap of her bag around her long fingers. 'I'm not going to do anything to jeopardise his chances of recovery.' She bit down hard on her lower lip. 'I suppose it all depends on Jake, doesn't it? How he—how he reacts when he sees me.'

Julie took a deep breath. 'I suppose so. Oh, God, I hope your arrival doesn't cause him to have a relapse. Why couldn't he have stayed where he was?'

Abby couldn't help wishing the same thing, but it was too late now. And, now that she was within minutes of seeing her son again, how could she be expected to turn back?

Iron gates stood wide at the entrance to Sandbar, but old Zeke Samuels was making an afternoon's work out of weeding the flower-beds just beyond the entrance, and he straightened his back to stare at them as the Jeep went by. He raised his trowel in a gesture of salute, but Julie's mouth tightened as they accelerated up the drive.

'It'll be a wonder if Jake doesn't know we're coming before we get there,' she muttered, swerving to avoid a sleek black cat that ran into their path. 'Get out of the way, Minerva!' she yelled, before continuing, 'People don't need a telephone around here. The local grapevine does equally as well. I'm telling you, the minute we were out of sight one or other of Zeke's grandchildren will

have been hurrying to carry the news, and if I know
Melinda she'll be blabbing it for anyone to hear.'

'Melinda.' Abby shook her head. 'Is she still here?'
Jake's West Indian housekeeper had seemed old when
Abby first came to Laguna Cay.

'Can you imagine her letting anyone else take over her
position?' demanded Julie, glad of the momentary
diversion. 'No, she's still here, even if her daughter
Rosabelle does most of the real work.'

'Rosabelle.'

'Hmm, did you meet her?'

'I'm not sure.' Abby frowned. 'Melinda had so many
relations.'

'Don't I know it?' Julie allowed a fleeting grin. 'Do
you remember? Jake let me take Ruby and Theresa home
to Florida. Well, they're both married now and raising
families of their own, and Melinda's got great-
grandchildren to add to her collection.'

Abby shared her smile, but the moment's relaxation
was brief. Already the cream-washed walls of Sandbar
were visible through the screen of palms and poinciana
trees that sheltered it from the road, and her nerves
tightened automatically at the prospect of what was to
come.

The two-storey villa was shaded in the late afternoon
sun, the shutters newly opened as the heat of the day
began to recede. Bougainvillaea clung to its outer walls,
climbing over the veranda, that looked very inviting at
this time of day, and stretching towards the iron-railed
balconies above. Some of the guest rooms were on this
side of the house, as well as the library, Jake's study,
and various other offices. But, as the building was built
Spanish-style around a central courtyard at the back,
most of the downstairs apartments opened into a cool,
tiled cloister. The views at the back of the house were
spectacular, Abby remembered, encompassing the whole
sweep of Oleander Bay. The suite of rooms she had

shared with Jake had occupied a prime position on the first floor, with its own shaded balcony overlooking the sparkling, sun-kissed water. She remembered it had had a bed, too, to match its surroundings—big, and impressive, and luxurious...

Julie brought the Jeep to a halt at the side of the house, where a huge flowering jacaranda cast a pool of darkness over the bleached stone path. The silence when the engine was switched off was broken only by the flutterings of wings above their heads as several doves were startled from their nesting place, and the steady hum of insects as they buzzed among the flowers.

Abby's nerves stretched. Had Jake heard the Jeep? she wondered. It was hardly possible that he couldn't have done so. Apart from the muted roar of the ocean on the reef, the air was as still and moist as a Turkish bath.

'Well, we're here,' said Julie unnecessarily, sliding out of the vehicle before leaning into the back to rescue Abby's suitcase. 'I wonder if Sara's got Dominic up from his nap yet.'

Abby swallowed. 'Sara?'

'Another of Melinda's grandchildren,' explained Julie, with a grimace. 'She took over as Dominic's nanny after Miss Napier handed in her notice. Didn't you know?'

'No.' Abby shook her head. 'Miss Napier's gone!' It hardly seemed possible. Jake had hired the spinsterish Miss Napier through an exclusive agency in London, and it was she who had escorted Dominic to London on those occasions when he had come to stay with his mother.

'Well, after Eve left, I don't think she felt comfortable living here alone with Jake,' replied Julie, her lips twitching. 'I don't know if she thought he was in danger of jumping on her or what, but she asked to be released from her contract.'

'Oh, God!' Abby couldn't prevent a smile in spite of her tension. The idea of Jake's being attracted to the middle-aged nanny was too ludicrous.

'I know.' Julie grinned in return. 'I'm surprised Jake didn't inform you.'

'Yes.' But Abby couldn't help thinking that this was one more reason why Dominic hadn't been allowed to come to England at Christmas.

The sound of footsteps on the path that ran around the side of the house momentarily arrested both thought and breathing, but the slap of bare feet against stone was less unnerving. And the man who came sauntering towards them was definitely not the father of her child, although his face was quite familiar.

'Oh, Joseph, I'm glad it's you,' said Julie on a gulp, revealing that she had been as tense as Abby. 'Um—take Miss Abby's things up to the first floor, will you? Rosa will tell you later where she wants them putting.'

'Yes, ma'am.' Joseph bent to pick up Abby's case and holdall, and then, with an astonished cry, he caught his first glimpse of their guest.

'Why—it's Miz Abby!' he exclaimed, dropping the case again, as his black lips parted delightedly over brilliant white teeth.

'I just said that,' said Julie drily, raising her eyebrows at Abby, but the black man wasn't paying her any attention.

'Miz Abby!' he declared, stepping over the discarded luggage, and coming to shake her hand. 'Well, you're a sight for sore eyes, and no mistake. Young Dominic's going to be real excited, when he finds out you're here.'

'I hope so.'

But Abby was nervous and it showed. Wiping a film of sweat from her upper lip, she wished she could have avoided this confrontation. But she had forgotten how relaxed the pace of life was at Sandbar, and Joseph's greeting was typical of his disregard for authority. Not

that it wasn't welcome, exactly, but she couldn't believe
it wasn't audible to everyone else in the house.

'Apparently the grapevine wasn't as efficient as I
thought,' murmured Julie, as Abby at last succeeded in
freeing herself from Joseph, and turned back to Jake's
sister. 'Come along.' She started along the path that
Joseph had used. 'We might as well go this way. I'd
guess that Jake is taking a rest.'

Smoothing her skirt as far over her legs as it would
go, Abby followed Julie along the flagged path. Through
a juniper hedge she could see the tennis-courts, and the
wall of the indoor squash court and gymnasium. These
buildings were set at a lower level than the house itself,
and out of sight of the courtyard and the veranda. The
swimming-pool was immediately below the house, a
curving expanse of green water, with vine-hung changing
cabanas, each with their own shower and vanity unit.
But she and Jake had invariably swum in the sea, she
remembered, the shallow waters, or *bajamar*, as the
Spaniards used to say, teeming with underwater life.

Following Julie round a corner now, Abby was confronted by the arching colonnade that circled the inner
walls of the house. Dappled shadows pooled on the
Italian tiles of the veranda, where urns of flowering
shrubs provided oases of colour, and, in the centre of
the courtyard, a playing fountain spilled its cooling
outflow into a carved stone basin. It was all exactly as
she remembered, and her heart caught in her throat at
the painful familiarity.

'Beautiful, isn't it?' murmured Julie wryly, aware of
her friend's reaction. 'Well—no one seems to be about,
thank goodness. Would you like to see your room first,
and freshen up?'

Abby thought she would like nothing better, but before
she could get her tongue around the words a shadow
moved beneath the colonnade. It was barely perceptible,
and with their eyes blinded by the sun Abby guessed

they were not presumed to notice. But with her heightened sensibilities any movement would have drawn her eyes, and her mouth dried expectantly as her knees turned to water.

'Julie,' she whispered anxiously, but Jake's sister was already crossing the flower-strewn courtyard, apparently unaware of being observed.

'Are you coming?' she demanded, turning back to address the other girl half impatiently, but Abby could only stare a warning as a dark-clad figure moved into the light.

Immediately, Abby came to a standstill. She had not been moving very fast anyway, but her unnatural stiffening at last apprised Julie that something was wrong. With a frown drawing her dark brows together, she slowed her step and turned questioningly towards the arched colonnade, only to stall abruptly as she recognised her brother.

For it was Jake, as Abby had known it had to be. Something, some extra sense perhaps, had alerted her to his presence long before he had taken the decision to step out into the sunlight. She had no idea what he was thinking, of course, but as their eyes met across the lengthening shadows of the courtyard she felt the same shuddering jolt of emotion she had first felt at a party in Manhattan almost eight years ago. It wasn't quite the same. Then, she had been a fairly unsophisticated newcomer to the world of photographic modelling, the trip to New York her first real taste of commercial success. But she felt the same sudden lurch of attraction, the same frightening absence of defence—the only thing that was different was that Max was no longer with her.

Yet, in spite of that initial surge of recognition, a second examination of the man standing only a dozen yards away from her promoted a different perspective. Although, as the man she had lived with for almost two years, he was unmistakable, he had perceptibly changed.

He had always been a tall man, topping her height by three or four inches, so that she was put in the unusual position of having to look up at him. But he had never been so thin, so gaunt, the skin stretching over his cheekbones and outlining the angular hollows of his face. His hair, too, once dark and crisp and cut neatly to the line of his collar, was now overlong and streaked with grey, framing his narrow features and accentuating his pallor. She knew he had been ill, yet, ridiculously, she had not expected him to look ill; but he did. Disturbingly so. And all her preconceptions about coming here were instantly dismissed.

CHAPTER TWO

'JAKE!' It was Julie who spoke first, gathering her composure, and continuing towards him. 'What—er—what are you doing out here? I thought you'd be resting.'

'Giving you the opportunity to smuggle that woman into my house without my knowledge, hmm?' Jake enquired, without heat, the dark gravelly voice that Abby remembered so well scraping over her nerves like a rough hand. 'I wondered where you'd got to. Rosa said you'd gone out in the Jeep.'

'Well, I did.' Julie was defensive. 'But I didn't intend to smuggle Abby into the house——'

'Didn't you?'

'No.'

'But you didn't tell me she was coming,' Jake observed moderately. 'I assume you did send for her. Does Dominic know she's here?'

'Of course not...' began Julie uneasily, and, realising it was up to her to come to the rescue, Abby straightened her spine and started towards them.

'Julie thought she was doing the right thing, Jake,' she declared, relieved to find her voice sounded confident anyway, even if she was shaking inside. 'You were in hospital, and she didn't know when you were coming home, and she couldn't go home herself and leave Dominic with no one to care for him.'

'Dominic has a nursemaid,' said Jake abruptly, his voice cooling perceptibly. 'There was no need for you to interrupt your schedule and come dashing out here. We can manage very well without you.'

26

Abby's nails dug into the palms of her hands as his cool, appraising gaze skimmed the creamy contours of her body with insolent deliberation. At least his eyes hadn't changed, she thought, as he lifted them to her face. Their gold-flecked brilliance was only lightly over-laid by a sombre cast. But, although he had used that look on her before, and to devastating effect, he was aware of her—though she guessed he'd never admit it. And, closer to, she was conscious that he had lost none of his disturbing sexuality. No one but Jake had ever stirred her senses in quite that way, and, despite her de-termination to meet him on his own terms, there was a forbidden temptation in seeing how far she could go.

'You forget,' she said now, meeting his gaze with annoying plausibility, 'Dominic is my son, too. If his father and—I hear—his stepmother are not here to look after him, then naturally I'm the obvious one to turn to.'

'And you are nothing if not *obvious*,' declared Jake harshly, drawing a protesting sound from his sister. 'Well, I'm sorry, but you've had a wasted journey. As you can see, I'm here now, and Dominic is in no danger of being neglected.'

Abby was not perturbed. For the first time in her life she felt as if they were meeting on equal terms, and it was an exhilarating experience.

But, for all she was enjoying herself, she had no wish to hurt Jake as he had once hurt her. And she was ever mindful of what Julie had told her about his illness. Until she knew a little more about it, she was not about to throw any weapons. But she did need to be allowed to stay.

'Julie tells me you and Eve have parted,' she remarked, watching a muscle in his cheek jerk spasmodically. 'What a shame! You never told me.'

'It was nothing to do with you,' said Jake shortly, but even though the sun was lower in the sky, and the heat of the day was giving way to a cooler dampness, there was a film of sweat on his forehead.

'I disagree.' Abby was polite. 'I should have been informed.'

'Why?' Jake shook off the detaining hand his sister laid on his arm. 'My divorce can be of no interest to you. You were not involved.'

'But I was.' Abby's voice was still pleasant, but courtesy was getting her nowhere. 'You must have known my solicitor would have been very interested in the news. Or were you planning on getting married again, before I could do anything about it?'

'You—*bitch*!'

'Bastard,' said Abby cordially, and Julie caught her breath.

'*Jake! Abby!*' She glared at both of them. 'Can't we at least go inside and discuss this?'

'There's nothing to discuss,' replied Jake heavily, running a hand, that Abby saw shook a little, through his hair. The hand came to rest at the nape of his neck, parting the lapels of his dark blue shirt and exposing the hollows gouged into his throat. It made him vulnerable somehow, more vulnerable than Abby would have deemed possible, and just for a moment her determination faltered. Dear God, she didn't want to upset him, she thought worriedly, realising Julie had not been exaggerating when she spoke about his weakness. But it wasn't her fault that he had kept the truth from her, and she didn't intend to leave here without spending some time with her son.

'Mummy! Mummy!'

The sound of running footsteps arrested all further thought, and Abby turned to see a small boy racing along the veranda towards them. A dark girl behind him looked as if she would have restrained him if she could, but it was too late. Dominic had seen his mother, and nothing was going to stop him reaching her.

In minute white shorts and matching T-shirt, his skin, that used to mirror his father's, tanned evenly over arms and legs that glowed with health, he charged into her arms. And Abby lifted him against her, burying her face in the scented hollow of his neck. There were tears in her eyes, but she didn't want him to see them. She loved him so much, and there was no way she was going to mar his delight in seeing her.

'Why didn't you let me know you were coming?' he demanded now, drawing back to look at her, his small hands sliding through her hair with painful familiarity. 'Daddy,' he swung round in her arms so that he could see his father, and continued his protest, 'did you know Mummy was coming? Why didn't I know about it?'

'Nobody knew about it, sugar,' said Abby firmly, ignoring Jake's grim features. 'I thought I'd surprise you—all of you,' she added, casting a defiant look over her shoulder. 'I'm glad you're pleased to see me. I'm very pleased to see you.'

'Shall we all go inside now?' suggested Julie, once again, looking at her brother with anxious appeal. 'Jake, you ought to be resting, whatever you say, and——' in a lowered tone that only he was supposed to hear '—there's no way you can expect Abby to leave tonight.'

But Abby heard, and so did Dominic, and he slid down from his mother's arms to confront his father with troubled eyes. 'Mummy's not leaving again, is she?' he protested, the throb of tears replacing his earlier excitement. As with any child of five, his emotions could swing swiftly from laughter to tears, and, as he looked down at his son, it seemed that Jake realised too how fragile trust could be.

'No,' he said, after a moment, though when he looked up and met Abby's cautious gaze his eyes were bleak. 'No, your mother isn't leaving for a little while,' he added. 'Perhaps you'd like to ask Rosa to make up a room for her. I'm sure she'd like to freshen up.'

* * *

The sound of the ocean woke her. That, and her body clock, reminding her that back in England it was already nearing noon. But here, on Laguna Cay, it was barely six-thirty in the morning, and the muted roar of the incoming tide splintering into foam on the reef was the only disturbance.

Sliding her legs over the side of the bed, Abby sat for a moment, head tilted back, shoulders raised, allowing the incredible knowledge of where she was and what she was doing to wash over her. Then, as the delicious coolness of the air inspired more energy, she rose to her feet and padded to the windows.

The rooms she had been given occupied a corner of the west wing of the house—well away from Jake's apartments, she had noted. Nevertheless, the view from her windows was just as spectacular, and, pressing down on the handle of the french doors, she stepped out on to her balcony.

The air was magical at this hour of the morning. Before the heat of the day sapped everything with moisture, the breeze carried only the perfumes of the flowers and the fragrance of the ocean. The air was warm, of course—as warm as a June day in London. But there was no smell of exhaust fumes here, no noxious crush of humanity. Only the promise of sunshine, and the lingering scent of the tropics.

And, although it was only two days since she left England, Abby could already feel herself adjusting to the climate. Although she hadn't thought about it at the time, her ferry ride the previous day had left a trace of colour on her skin, and, examining the damage, she guessed she'd have to be more careful in the future. The fact that she had the kind of skin that welcomed the sun's rays would be of no cheer to her agent. Bearing in mind that Marcia had plans for her to model winter fashions when she got back, she must avoid too much exposure. Leathers and sables did not look well against sun-tanned flesh.

All the same, she couldn't deny the sense of well-being that came from soaking up the sun's rays. Indeed, she liked nothing better than stretching out in her bikini and basking in the heat. She would just have to make sure she smothered herself in sun-screen. With a little care, it shouldn't be a problem.

The breeze wafted under the hem of her thigh-length cotton nightshirt, and she moved her legs defensively. The trouble was, she was adapting too well to the climate, she thought ruefully. Still, until the sun got higher, she couldn't suppress a shiver.

She was on the point of going back into her room when she saw him. Beyond the pool, and the colourful shrubs that surrounded it, the sand fell away towards the shoreline. The beach itself curved like a sickle around the contours of the bay, with only a few waving palm trees casting shadows like fingers pointing towards the sea. She guessed Jake's shadow had blended in with the rest, and, as she had not expected to see anyone about at this hour of the morning, she had not paid proper attention. But now he was walking towards the water, and his identity was unmistakable.

Abby stepped back abruptly, her pulse racing out of control. How long had Jake been down there? she wondered. What was he doing? Had he seen her, and thought she was watching him? Or was he as completely indifferent to her presence as he would like her to think?

She took a deep breath. It was the first time she had seen him since they had parted on the veranda the afternoon before. Dominic had been afraid to let her out of his sight, it seemed, and he had insisted she accompany him to find Rosabelle, the acting housekeeper. For, although Melinda was ostensibly in charge, as Julie had said, it was her daughter who did most of the work.

As it happened, Abby hadn't seen Melinda either. Rosabelle, or Rosa, as she was usually called, had explained that her mother was visiting another daughter and her family at the other side of the island, and wouldn't be back until after supper.

'But she'll sure be glad to see you again, Miz Abby,' Rosa insisted, as she escorted them upstairs. 'She never did take to Mrs Lowell, you know. She often talks about the time when you and Mr Jake lived here together. Those were happy times. Yes, indeed. She'll be real pleased to see you're back.'

'I'm not back, Rosa.' Abby felt obliged to make some explanation. 'I mean—well, I am. At the moment. But not for long——'

'Well, you are here now, aren't you?' Rosa declared simply, turning to wait for Dominic, who was climbing the stairs behind them. 'And that's what matters, I'm sure. Isn't that right, young man?'

Of course, Dominic had agreed, particularly as Abby had been persuaded to supervise his bath, and then she had stayed with him while he'd had his supper in the nursery. Jake had designed a suite of attractive apartments for his son, with every kind of game and toy imaginable to keep him entertained. But Abby had wondered what role his stepmother had played in the boy's life if he had needed so many diversions.

She had waited while Dominic had gone to say goodnight to his father, and then tucked him up in the pint-sized bed that had been built especially for him. She didn't ask him what he had said to his father, or indeed what his father had said to him. But she had gone downstairs afterwards, firmly convinced she was going to find out.

However, Jake had not put in an appearance. Only Julie was there to explain that he had gone to bed too, obliged, much against his will, she added, to take the rest he badly needed.

'You had me worried earlier on,' she continued, picking at the aromatic fish stew which Rosabelle had served for dinner. 'I honestly thought, after all this time, you and Jake could have met one another without hostility. Instead of which, you couldn't wait to snipe at one another. I really thought you had more sense.'

'Who? Me?' Abby asked quietly, and Julie sighed.

'Oh—both of you, I suppose,' she admitted fairly. 'Just—be careful, will you? I love my brother very much, and I don't want to feel responsible if he gets hurt.'

Well, she didn't want to hurt him either, thought Abby now, dragging her eyes away from the figure on the beach, and turning to survey the room behind her. But that didn't mean she intended to ignore him. Jake had her son, and until that particular problem was resolved there was no way she was going to avoid it.

Now, she tugged the skimpy nightshirt over her head and tossed it on to the foot of the bed. The huge iron-railed four-poster had proven just as comfortable as it looked, and she linked her fingers and stretched them luxuriously over her head as she strode into the bathroom.

The shower was appealing, but she decided it would take too long. For the moment, she contented herself with cleaning her teeth in the peach-tinted basin, and then sluiced her face with warm water. Time enough for a shower later. Right now she would never have a better chance of talking to Jake alone.

She scarcely gave a glance to the bedroom as she stepped into green and white striped shorts and a green cotton halter. She had admired its cream and gold luxury the night before, endeavouring to share Dominic's enthusiasm as he scampered from room to room. But the fruitwood desk and the velvet-seated chairs in the sitting-room, and the pale silk walls and flower-printed curtains in the bedroom, had actually meant very little to her. She was no longer seduced by possessions, she reflected, remembering the innocent she used to be. Once she had thought you couldn't fail to be happy in such surroundings. But life had taught her differently, and she wasn't likely to forget.

She took a moment to study her reflection before leaving her apartments. She looked different, too, she thought, from the way she had looked before. Her hair, that had always been a honey-brown in colour, and which had once been long enough to touch her hips, was now no more than shoulder-length. It was presently crimped, and streaked with silver, framing her face with its fullness, and deepening the blue colour of her eyes. Below a fringe of silky lashes, her cheekbones framed the perfect oval of her face, and her mouth, the lower lip fuller than the upper, was generously wide and mobile.

Her features hadn't changed, she decided, except perhaps that they had matured. After all, she was now twenty-eight. But she was slimmer, even if her breasts were still a source of some contention between her and Marcia. For, no matter how little she ate, they persistently remained just a touch too generous, spilling out of swimwear with a total disregard for fashion.

She sighed, wondering how Jake saw her now, and whether his first thought was still of her and Max. Of course, it must be, she reflected, pressing her lips together with sudden frustration. The way he had looked at her the previous afternoon had been evidence of his feelings. And, no matter how physically attracted he might be to her flawless body, his mind would still see the corruption of her soul.

The thought made her feel restless. Was that the only memory Jake had of their time together? It might be interesting to find out. What did she have to lose, after all? He had already taken everything she had ever loved from her.

After sliding her feet into canvas shoes, she opened her bedroom door into the corridor beyond. Although it was daylight, bronze-shaded lamps burned constantly along these innner hallways, reflecting in the polished wood floors, and gilding the various vases and sculptures that were set between the doors. There were rugs on the floor, soft white oriental rugs that cushioned her feet, like a sponge. And mirrors to add illumination— and images of herself, she would rather not see.

The corridor led to a galleried landing, and she paused at the head of the curving staircase, looking down into the hall below. But there was no evidence of any activity and, running silently down the stairs, she let herself out on to the veranda.

The air was still as delightful as it had been earlier, perhaps a little warmer now, but just as fresh and delicious. Leaving the veranda, she emerged into the sunlight, and then swiftly crossed the courtyard and descended the steps to the swimming-pool.

The water was inviting, but she didn't give it a second look. Her eyes had already identified their objective some distance away, along the shore, and, shunning the tropical gardens, she stepped on to the sand.

The temptation to remove her shoes and allow the warm, clear water to cool her toes was almost irresistible, but she suppressed it. At the moment, she had the advantage, in that Jake had not yet seen her. If she stopped to paddle, he would be bound to notice her.

As it was, he seemed to sense her approach before she reached him. She was still several yards away when he turned and saw her. In consequence, she had no way of knowing what his initial reaction had been. By the time she reached him, his features were rigidly controlled.

Like her, he was wearing shorts this morning, worn denim cut-offs that hung low on his narrow hips and exposed the muscled length of his legs. The shirt, which he had been wearing when she saw him from her balcony,

was now slung about his neck for coolness, but her eyes
were drawn to the fine dark hair that arrowed down to
his navel.

She guessed he would have preferred them to meet in
less casual circumstances. Despite his air of indifference, there was a definite tightness about his lips that
revealed his irritation. Still, he seemed to accept that there
was nothing he could do about it, and, likewise, he had
no intention of showing how he really felt.

'Good morning,' she said brightly, determined not to
let him gain the upper hand, and he ran an exploring
hand over the overnight's growth of beard on his jawline.
The darkness of his beard threw the sallowness of his
skin into sharp relief, but the golden eyes were steady,
and filled with raw dislike.

'Is it?'

'I think so,' she declared, refusing to be daunted.
'Mmm,' she lifted her shoulders, knowing that as she
did so her breasts swelled against the soft fabric of her
halter, 'this is such a marvelous place! I'd forgotten how
beautiful it was.'

Jake averted his eyes from the sight of her nipples,
outlined by the thin cloth, and said harshly, 'Just why
did you come here, Abby? You must have known you
wouldn't be welcome. This is my home, not a hotel. If
you were so concerned about Dominic, why didn't you
contact my solicitor?'

Abby took a breath before replying. 'I came because
I wanted to see my son,' she said simply. 'And, unlike
you, I don't enjoy dealing through a third party. Why
shouldn't I come and see him? You may have custody,
but I have access.'

'I've never denied you that, have I?' Jake's voice was
bitter. 'As a matter of fact, I've always made it easy for
you. Dominic has been escorted to England with rig-
orous regularity.'

'Until last Christmas,' Abby reminded him smoothly. 'Why didn't you let Dominic come to London then, Jake? Were you afraid he might tell me Eve had gone?'

'Don't be ridiculous!' Jake looked at her then, his eyes darkening angrily. 'He had a cold. I told you. Or at least my solicitor did. Whatever the circumstances, he was not fit to travel. Children do suffer from colds, you know. Even here.'

Abby shrugged, taking the few steps that brought her to the water's edge. Then, bending, she took off her shoes and stepped into the shallows. The silky rivulets of lace-edged sea-water were cooler than she had expected, and she shivered. But her awareness of the angry man behind her prevented her from enjoying the experience.

As if compelled against his will, Jake moved to stand beside her, his bare feet splashing her legs as he stamped into the water. 'Just tell me,' he said, grasping her bare arm above the elbow to attract her attention, 'how long do you think you're going to stay here?'

There was nothing weak about the fingers that gripped her flesh, and Abby looked down at them circling her arm with unexpected emotion. He was hurting her, but he seemed completely unaware of that. 'As long as you'll let me, I suppose,' she answered softly, turning her head so that her face was only inches from his own. 'Unless you're prepared to let me take Dominic back to London, of course.' Her tongue appeared and moistened her lips. 'I'm afraid that's the only alternative.'

Jake swore then, harshly but distinctly, releasing her arm with a disgusted gesture, as if he had just become aware of what he was doing. 'And what if I don't accept either of those alternatives?' he retorted, gazing at her coldly. 'What are you going to do about it? Dominic lives here.'

'For the present,' said Abby pleasantly, forced to make her point. 'But a judge might view your circumstances differently, now that your—wife—has left you.'

He stared at her for another long minute, and then abruptly turned away, leaving Abby feeling bruised and unsteady. But it wasn't the physical pain he had inflicted that had dried her mouth and quickened her pulse. It was the knowledge that he could still do this to her that distressed her. But he wasn't going to know it. Not if she could help it.

It was Jake's own shallow breathing that brought her round to face him, however. The unnatural sound at each intake of air chilled her blood, and she gazed at him in horror. He had stumbled a few yards further along the beach, but was bent over, fighting for every breath, his colour non-existent, sweat pouring from him.

'Oh, God!' she breathed, trying not to panic, but it wasn't easy. The house seemed miles away from where they were standing, and the isolation she had previously welcomed was now a worrying reality. If only she could see somebody, she thought. If only Zeke or Joseph, or even Rosabelle, was about. Between them, they could surely have carried Jake back.

As if, even in his present state, Jake could sense her distress, he struggled into speech. 'I'm all right——'

'Like hell, you are!' retorted Abby sharply, and then, realising how insensitive that might sound, she shook her head. 'I mean—oh, you know what I mean. You shouldn't have walked so far.'

Jake made a negative gesture with his hand, panting as he dragged air into his lungs. Each agonised breath was like a knife, scraping a layer of skin from her body, exposing her own vulnerability where Jake Lowell was concerned.

She wanted to help him, but what could she do? She had no medical skills; she had never even attended a class in first aid. All she could do was stand staring at him, willing some all-powerful deity to come and save them both. She dared not leave him. The time it would take for her to run to the house and get help might be crucial. Somehow, she had the feeling that, so long as she was with him, he wouldn't die. But if she left him alone...

Was his breathing getting easier? Watching him, she thought perhaps it was. There was not that harsh grating sound with every laboured breath, and, although his hands were still braced on his knees, what she saw as his struggle for survival did not seem so pronounced.

'Jake...'

She tested his name on her tongue, moving tentatively towards him, and laying a hand on his shoulder. His flesh was damp, and cooler than it should have been, but the firm texture of his skin beneath her fingers was marvellously reassuring. She wanted to put her arms about him then. She wanted to hold him close, and comfort him, and tell him she was sorry for causing him to have this attack. Her relief that he seemed to be recovering was making her feel weak and light-headed, and she was in imminent danger of betraying emotions that had no place in this affair.

But—probably wisely, she decided later—Jake was experiencing no such softening. With a muffled oath, he moved, so that she was forced to drop her hand, regarding her now with frustrated eyes as he fought to regain his composure.

'I'm not dying,' he said, through tight lips. 'I just— swallowed my breath, that's all.'

Abby didn't believe him, but she wasn't about to start another argument. 'If you say so,' she murmured, wiping her damp palms down the seams of her shorts. 'But—I think we ought to be getting back.'

'You can do what the hell you like,' returned Jake unevenly, straightening up cautiously, and then flexing his shoulder muscles with evident relief. 'I'll come back when I'm good and ready. I'm not an invalid, so stop treating me like one.'

This was patently so untrue that Abby could only stare at him, and, with a latent sense of honesty, Jake groaned. 'Well, OK,' he admitted wearily, 'I have not been well. But it's nothing serious. Just overwork, that's all. So long as I take it easy for a while, I'll be fine.'

'But you're not taking it easy, are you?' Abby murmured, unable to prevent the criticism. 'Julie says you've hardly been off the phone since you got home.'

'Julie should mind her own bloody business,' returned Jake feelingly. 'And I can't just abandon the corporation, can I? We're in the middle of take-over negotiations for the Harold Hadley group. I need to know what's happening. There's got to be no slip-ups.'

'Why should there be?' Abby sighed. 'What about Raymond Walker? Doesn't he work for you any more?'

'Ray? Sure, he still works for the company.'

'Then why can't he handle the negotiations? You used to say he knew your job almost as well as you did.'

Jake seemed to consider what she had said for a moment, and then, as if he realised who it was offering him advice, his mouth compressed. 'I'll make my own decisions about who can, or can't, handle this deal,' he declared coldly. 'Just get off my back, will you? I don't need your opinion, period.'

Abby turned away then, unexpectedly stung by his harsh words. It was what she should have expected, she knew, but just for a moment his cruel tongue hurt. She was still too sensitive, she realised. Exposed by her own sympathy for him. But keep it up, she told him silently. It was easier to hate him when he didn't seem so vulnerable.

She glanced back to find him scowling at the incoming tide, and just for a moment her heart ached. But then she forced herself to remember how he had taken Dominic away from her, and any lingering sympathy she felt for him evaporated on the breeze. That didn't mean she'd take any unnecessary chances with his health, she reminded herself firmly. But she wasn't going to disappear just because he said so.

CHAPTER THREE

ABBY was having breakfast on the veranda when
Dominic appeared.

She wasn't particularly hungry, especially after returning to the house alone. But Rosabelle had insisted
on providing her with freshly squeezed orange juice and
newly baked croissants, and she couldn't disappoint the
housekeeper by refusing the delicious food. Besides, the
strong Columbian coffee Rosa served with the meal had
marvellous restorative qualities. Abby had drunk three
cups already. She could feel the caffeine inside her now,
working on her overtaxed nerves, and she refused to
think of Marcia and what she had said stimulants did
to Abby's complexion.

The advent of her son was a welcome diversion,
however. It was wonderful to have him rush into her
arms again, as he had done the night before, and his
uncomplicated affection was all the compensation she
needed. *He* was the reason she had come here, she reminded herself severely. Jake's illness was just a con-
tributing factor.

Rosa reappeared as Abby was introducing herself to
Dominic's nursemaid. The dark girl Abby had only
glimpsed the night before was less intimidated now that
Jake was not around, and she was not so willing to
abandon her charge to Abby's ministrations. Abby
guessed she had been told that she was Dominic's
mother, but that was all. And Sara—as she was called—
apparently took her duties seriously.

However, Rosa had no such reservations. 'You can
leave the boy with Miz Abby,' she declared, instantly

weighing up the situation. 'Ain't no sense in you hanging about here this morning. You go find Henrietta. She find something else for you to do.'

Sara went, albeit unwillingly, and Abby hoped she hadn't made another enemy. But over the years she had had so little time with Dominic, and she couldn't give up this opportunity, not even to please the nursemaid.

Rosa provided fresh milk and cornflakes for the little boy, and Abby thought how pleasant it was, sharing the meal with her son. He was older now, more capable of conducting a proper conversation, and he was innocently eager to talk about his father.

'He is going to be all right now, isn't he?' he asked, pausing, with a spoonful of cereal halfway to his mouth, and Abby sighed.

'I'm sure he is,' she said quickly, not wanting to dwell on that aspect of the situation. 'Your daddy's a strong man. He just needs to rest more, that's all.'

Dominic absorbed this in silence for a moment, and then he frowned. 'What would I do if Daddy wasn't here?' he asked. 'Would I come to live with you, or would I have to stay with Grandma Lowell?'

Abby took a careful breath. 'As that's not likely to happen——'

'But if it did?'

Abby put down the knife she had been using to spread butter on a croissant, and was annoyed to find her hand was trembling. 'I don't think we should consider such a possibility,' she declared, helping herself to more coffee. 'Um—do you see much of—Grandma Lowell? Does she come to stay on the island?'

'Not usually,' replied Dominic, resting his elbow on the table, and propping his head on his hand. He swirled the remaining milk round in his bowl, and grimaced. 'I go to stay with her sometimes. I went there when Aunt Eve went away.'

Aunt Eve! Abby caught her lower lip between her teeth. It was a yawning temptation to ask her son about his stepmother's departure. She wouldn't have been human if she hadn't been curious about what happened.

Still, she controlled the impulse for the moment, and thought instead about Jake's mother. Mrs Lowell lived in Florida, like her daughter. A widow now, she was as English as Abby herself, but she had married an American, Jake's father, and she much preferred the warmth of Palm Beach to the damper climate of London. Abby couldn't say she knew her well. She had lived with Jake for almost two years, and she had only seen her perhaps half a dozen times. But, after Abby had had her baby, it was Mrs Lowell who had flown to London to bring Dominic back to Laguna Cay, and for this reason, if for no other, Abby had come to dislike her.

Realising that Dominic was watching her now with a dark and troubled stare, Abby forced a smile to her lips. 'Elbows off the table,' she said lightly, making him sit up. 'What are we going to do this morning? Would you like to go for a walk or what?'

'Don't you want me to come and live with you?'

Dominic's queston was as unexpected as it was solemn, and Abby sucked in her breath. 'Why—of course I do——'

'But I don't live with you, do I? I live with Daddy. And he's almost never here.'

There was a plaintive note in his voice now, and Abby didn't quite know how to answer him. The last thing she had expected was that Dominic might not be happy here. But he was getting older all the time, and perhaps he needed the companionship of children of his own age.

'I—suppose you miss Aunt Eve,' she ventured at last, loath to bring up Jake's ex-wife, but needing to know something more about the relationship between her son and his stepmother. 'Were you sad when she went away?'

'Not likely.' Dominic wrinkled his nose. 'I was glad!'

'Glad?' Abby was both surprised and, undeniably, pleased.

'Yes, glad.' Dominic hunched his shoulders, and propped both elbows on the table now. 'All she and Daddy did was fight all the time.'

'Did they?' Abby's tongue touched her upper lip.

'She didn't like it here,' went on Dominic confidentially, and, although Abby knew she ought to stop him, she didn't. 'She liked it best when Daddy went away and took her with him. She said the island was boring.'

'I see.'

Dominic frowned suddenly. 'Did you get bored?' he asked. 'Melinda said you used to live here, before I was born. Why did you go away?'

'Oh . . .' Abby found that question harder to answer. 'Well, I—had to work, you see. And there are no modelling jobs on Laguna Cay.'

Dominic did not look convinced. 'Did you fight, too?' he pondered, his small fists cupping his chin. 'Is that why you and Daddy don't live together like other mummies and daddies do?'

Abby decided this catechism had gone far enough. She had no answer for him. None that his small intelligence could comprehend, anyway. The reasons she had left Laguna Cay would have to wait until he was much older. She only hoped he would understand her failings better than his father had done.

Julie appeared as they were leaving the breakfast table. Today, Jake's sister was wearing heels and a floral sundress, and Abby raised her dark brows at the obviously more formal attire.

'I'm leaving this morning,' said Julie, by way of an explanation. 'Bob Fletcher's flying out from Nassau to pick me up, and I'll take the shuttle from Nassau to Miami.'

'Oh.' Abby felt suddenly anxious. 'Are you sure?'

'Sure about what?' Julie took the chair Abby had just vacated, and helped herself to a cup of coffee. 'Sure about Bob bringing the chopper over, or sure about taking the shuttle to Miami?'

'You know what I mean.' Abby glanced down at Dominic, but he was happily chasing a butterfly around the courtyard. 'Is it wise to leave me here with Jake?' she added, mouthing the words.

Julie shrugged. 'I don't know.'

'Well, then——'

'I can't stay indefinitely, Abby.' Julie put down her cup and looked up at the other girl. 'I'm not exactly happy about the situation myself, but I look at it this way: it's your life. Yours, and my brother's. You've got to make your own decisions. I can't stay here as a kind of—referee.'

'But he wasn't well this morning!' exclaimed Abby in a low voice. 'I—well, I joined him on the beach earlier, and he—he kind of—couldn't breathe.'

'What?' Julie frowned. 'When he saw you?'

'No.' Abby sighed in impatience. 'No. It was later. After we had talked.'

'Do you mean argued?' suggested Julie drily, and, seeing the faint colour that invaded the other girl's cheeks, she shook her head. 'It happens,' she said. 'If he gets uptight about anything, he loses control of his breathing. According to the doctor, it's just another symptom of his condition. It exhausts him, but he eventually recovers.'

'But—that's terrible!'

'I did warn you.'

'Not about that.'

Julie sighed now. 'Jake collapsed, Abby,' she said quietly. 'No one really knows why. It was a combination of a lot of things, not least the fact that he doesn't eat properly, he doesn't sleep properly, and he's constantly at the mercy of any cock-up that affects the corporation.

The doctors think his heart may have faltered, but there's no real evidence of heart damage, thank goodness. However, what he needs now is complete rest and total isolation. Time to give his body a chance to recover. At a guess, I'd say he's been living on the edge of something like this for a couple of years. Maybe longer. But he doesn't take any notice of me. I warned him again last night, after that little scene on the veranda, but he simply doesn't want to know. As far as Jake's concerned, I'm surplus to requirements now that he's home again, so I'm going. Honestly, Abby, *I* can't take any more.'

Abby gasped. 'Well, you can't imagine he'll take any notice of me!'

'Who knows?' Julie turned back to her coffee. 'You used to be able to wrap him round your little finger. No one else has ever been able to do that. Perhaps you'll be able to do it again.'

Abby stared at Julie's bent head. 'After yesterday afternoon, you can say that!'

'Well, you have to admit, he's not indifferent to you,' murmured Julie slyly. She looked up. 'Do your best, Abby. Try and make him show some sense.'

They heard the sound of the helicopter as they were paddling in the rock pools close to the headland. The sleek executive aircraft, with the logo of the Lowell Corporation emblazoned on its side, swung wide over the island, before dropping down to land near the house. The last time Abby had seen the company helicopter was the morning six years ago when she had left the island. Not the same helicopter, of course, but one similar, and she couldn't prevent a shiver at the remembrance of how she had felt.

Dominic, who had been quite content to poke about among the rocks, now looked up with anxious eyes. 'That's Daddy's 'copter,' he said.

'Yes.' Abby made a determined effort not to show any interest. 'Oh, look, isn't this shell pretty? What do you think it is?'

'He's not going away, is he?' Dominic stepped out of the rock pool and shaded his eyes. Although the helicopter was now out of sight, he continued to look towards the sky.

So much for his not being happy with his father, thought Abby drily, and wiped her wet hands on her shorts. 'No, he's not going away,' she assured her son firmly. 'The helicopter's come to take Aunt Julie back to Nassau, so she can get a plane home to Miami. She's going to see Uncle David, and Penny. I expect they've been wondering when she was coming back.'

'And Ruth,' said Dominic pedantically, and Abby hesitated only a moment before nodding.

'And Ruth,' she agreed, deciding not to go into the fact that his elder cousin was away at boarding school. The last thing she wanted was to put any worrying ideas into his head, particularly at this time.

Dominic pursed his lips. 'It's Daddy's 'copter,' he said again, still not convinced that his father was not going to use it. 'Uncle Bob us'lly flies it, but Daddy can fly it, too.'

'I know.' Abby sighed. 'But he's not using it today, honestly. When we get back from our walk, you can see for yourself.'

'He won't go while we're out, will he?' Dominic persisted, and Abby shook her head.

'Your father's been ill, sweetheart. He's not likely to be going anywhere for quite some time.' Although how true that was, she couldn't honestly say.

Dominic frowned. 'But he is better now, isn't he?' he asked. 'Aunt Julie said he was in hospital, but he wasn't. He came home.'

'Yes, well——' Abby didn't quite know how to answer that '—you know what your daddy's like. He thinks he knows better than the doctors. But we'll have to see he doesn't do anything silly.'

'How silly?'

Dominic was too precise, and Abby took a deep breath. 'Oh—we'll just have to make sure he takes things easy,' she declared, realising it wasn't always easy re-assuring a five-year-old.

The helicopter left again before they got back to the house, and Abby could sense Dominic's anxiety as he ran the last few yards along the beach. She guessed he wouldn't be satisfied until he actually saw his father for himself.

The area around the pool was deserted, the only occupants the birds, who skimmed in and out of the bushes and scattered petals on the marble tiles. The water in the pool reflected the veined marble beneath the surface, giving it a delicate greenness that was irre-sistibly inviting.

But Dominic paid no attention to the pool or the gaily striped sun-loungers, with their lightly twirling um-brellas. Without even awarding them a passing glance, he climbed the steps to the sun-splashed courtyard, and dived into the shade of the veranda with a careless familiarity.

There was no sign of Jake, but Abby refused to be disturbed. He wouldn't—he *couldn't*—have been so foolish as to accompany Julie back to the mainland. After what had happened this morning, she was quite prepared to believe what Julie had said. She had heard of high-powered businessmen cracking up before. And just because Jake was barely forty, there was no reason to suppose he was immune.

All the same, she knew how stubborn Jake could be. And no one—but no one—had ever been able to give him orders. It would be just like him to use her being here to his own advantage, she fretted nervously. Dear

God, he might even have used her presence as an excuse
to leave.

'Here he is!'

Dominic's singsong announcement came as almost a
relief. But, with the sun still blinding her eyes, it wasn't
easy to focus on the man who came out of the shadows
of the veranda carrying his son. She could see the shorts
he had worn on the beach earlier, and the cotton shirt
was now covering his torso. But his expression was less
easy to interpret, although his appearance was undeniably reassuring.

'Did you enjoy your walk?' Jake asked politely, and
Abby guessed he was making an effort to be civil in front
of the boy.

'Very much,' she answered, directing her smile at
Dominic. 'And now, if you don't mind, I'll go and put
on a swimsuit. Are you going to join me in the pool?'

Her question was to Dominic, but Jake evidently
sensed the challenge in her words. 'Not today,' he
declared, bending to set Dominic on his feet, and then
pulling a face at him when his son began to protest.
'Uncle Bob brought me some papers to look over,' he
continued. 'You—you and—Mummy have fun.' It was
obviously an effort to acknowledge her parentage. 'I'll
see you later. Probably at lunch.'

Dominic followed Abby upstairs. Now that he was sure
that his father was not planning on leaving, he seemed
more relaxed, though Abby sensed he wasn't totally at
ease. And how could she blame him? she wondered,
rummaging in her suitcase for the mechanical dog she
had bought for him in England. She had planned to give
it to him when they boarded the plane for the long flight
to London, but as that seemed less of a possibility now
she decided there was no point in hanging on to it.
Besides, it gave her a great deal of pleasure to watch his
delight when he discovered that the fluffy poodle could

do backflips as well as bark. And she thought he needed a diversion, after his earlier show of panic.

He was such a pitiful child in some ways, she worried. He had every material advantage, it was true, but it obviously wasn't enough. Oh, he loved his father. There was no doubt about that. And Jake loved him too, although perhaps his way of showing it was different. However, Dominic lived with the constant uncertainty of not knowing when Jake might go away and leave him, and without Miss Napier's stabilising influence he had lost the only security he had known.

Eve's departure would not have helped. However little he had cared for his stepmother, she had been another major fixture in his life. With no female figure now to identify with, no wonder he clung so desperately to his father. Had Jake any idea of the extent of his responsibility? Did he realise how important it was to Dominic that he should take no chances with his health?

Abby left Dominic playing with the dog while she went to put on her bikini. She, too, was only just beginning to understand the importance of her role in her son's eyes, and the knowledge that in less than a week she was due back in England was an added complication. Until now she had considered that the only obstacle to her plans was Jake. But, whether she stayed here on the island or took her son back to London, she had to accept that she had responsibilities, too.

Dominic was still playing with the toy when she emerged from the bathroom. But he scrambled to his feet when he saw her, his eyes widening admiringly as he took in her pale-skinned appearance.

'You look pretty,' he said, and Abby bent to give him a swift hug.

'Thank you, kind sir,' she smiled, though her expression sobered a little when she caught a glimpse of herself in the mirror. When she had packed the skimpy pink bikini, she had not expected anyone but her son to

see her. But it was the only swimsuit she had brought
with her, and Jake had seen her in less, of course.

But, that was many moons ago, she reminded herself
succinctly. Still, in the early days, she used to model
swimwear. Surely she could stand another pair of eyes
upon her? If she steeled herself sufficiently, she was sure
she could cope with anything.

Nevertheless, she slipped a sleeveless silk tabard over
the bikini. The loose tunic, in psychedelic shades of pink
and purple, just reached the tops of her legs, the sides
split almost to the waist to reveal the toning bikini briefs.

It was very peaceful beside the pool. Abby, who had
remembered to bring her skin cream, spread it liberally
over her arms and legs before settling herself on one of
the sun-loungers. With an umbrella tilted to shield her
face she couldn't deny a reluctant feeling of well-being.
Even the knowledge that Jake was in the house, only a
few yards away from her, couldn't prevent her sense of
enjoyment. She would have to think about what she was
going to do about Dominic later. For the present, she
was content to drift.

'Are you going to come in the pool?' Dominic asked
now, shedding his T-shirt on to the adjoining couch. Like
his father's, his skin could stand the brilliant heat of the
sun without burning. His small body was golden brown
and healthy, his limbs strong and sturdy without being
fat.

'Later,' said Abby comfortably, slanting a grey-blue
gaze in his direction. She summoned a lazy smile.
'Wouldn't you like to sit for a while before we go
swimming?'

Dominic hesitated for a moment, and then he perched
on the edge of the lounger beside her. 'Why do you put
that stuff on you?' he asked, touching the glistening skin
on Abby's arm. 'Don't you like the sun?'

'I like the sun, but the sun doesn't like me,' replied Abby ruefully. 'Or, at least, it makes my skin go red. Which isn't very nice.'

'Why not?'

'Well, because it makes my skin sore.'

'Don't you go brown?'

Abby sighed. 'I would. Eventually.'

'So why don't you?'

Abby bit her lip. 'Because I can't.'

'Why can't you?'

Abby regarded him doubtfully. 'Well—you know that Mummy models clothes, don't you?'

'You put on pretty dresses and get photographed,' said Dominic nodding. 'Yes. I've seen pictures of you.'

'Have you?' Abby frowned. She didn't remember showing him any.

'Yes. Daddy showed me.'

'*Daddy* showed you?'

'Yes. I asked him what you did, and he showed me some pictures.'

'Oh. Oh, I see.' Abby guessed Jake had borrowed some magazines from his mother for the purpose. 'Well, that's why I can't sit in the sun without putting cream on my skin. Brown skin doesn't look good on camera.'

'Mmm.'

Happily, this answer seemed to satisfy him for the moment, and she was relieved he didn't ask her any more questions. She had been dreading the one about how long she was staying. For the moment, she didn't even want to think about that.

Still, Dominic was restless, and eventually Abby agreed to go into the pool. It was something she wanted to do, after all, and she consoled herself with the thought that if she stayed underwater she might just avoid overexposure.

And it was delightful to cool her sticky limbs in the deep, clear water. With lazy strokes, she swam from one end of the pool to the other, and back again, before reaching for the bottom. It made her realise how much she had missed her daily work-out at the health club, back in Fulham. Even three days without exercise, and her muscles felt the strain.

Dominic surfaced beside her as she swept her hair out of her eyes. He was a good swimmer, having been taught by his father even before he could walk. Abby remembered that when she and Jake had talked about having a family Jake had declared that teaching a baby to swim would be a first priority. With the pool, and the ocean on the doorstep, it was imperative that their child should be safe in the water.

Of course, she hadn't been around to watch him do it, Abby reflected, a little bitterly now. Until Dominic was two years old, she had only seen him on very rare occasions. Jake had considered her lifestyle unsuitable for his son. And he still did, she acknowledged, choking realistically when Dominic climbed on her back and ducked her under the water. But the difference now was that Dominic *knew* he had two parents. And, no matter how objectionable that awareness must be to Jake, he was forced to acknowledge it too.

The sound of someone's feet descending the steps to the pool deck eventually reminded Abby that the sun was almost overhead. She and Dominic had been having so much fun in the water, she had forgotten she was supposed to be protecting her shoulders, and she scrambled out of the pool instinctively, barely glancing at the dark-skinned woman carrying a tray.

'Well, now, is that any way to treat an old friend?' demanded the woman peevishly, as Abby snatched up a towel from the linen trolley and, turning her back, began rubbing herself dry. She set down the tray of iced fruit juice on the table beside Abby's lounger, and put her hands on her hips. 'And I thought you'd be pleased to see me,' she added. 'Instead of which, you can't even say hello.'

Abby swung round disbelievingly. 'Melinda?' she exclaimed. 'Oh, Melinda, I didn't realise it was you.'

'I should hope not,' declared the old black woman reprovingly. She stared at Abby with evident affection. 'Lord, it's good to see you again, woman! I was beginning to think you'd forgotten where we lived.'

'Oh, Melinda!'

Abandoning the towel where it fell, Abby crossed the marbled tiles and felt herself enfolded in a warm embrace. Of all the servants at Sandbar, she had always loved Melinda the best, and the garrulous old housekeeper had been the only person, apart from Abby herself, who had dared to stand up to Jake and tell him what she thought.

'Well, then,' Melinda murmured at last, her voice suspiciously husky as she pushed Abby away from her. She fumbled in the pocket of her apron, and brought out a snow-white handkerchief to dab her eyes. 'Isn't this a fine thing?'

Abby felt suspiciously near to tears, too, but Dominic had climbed out of the water now, and was standing watching them with unconcealed curiosity. It made her realise that he might misunderstand her emotion, and, making a play of rescuing her towel, she surreptitiously wiped her misty lashes. 'So—how are you?' she asked.

'I'm all right.' Melinda ruffled Dominic's damp hair. 'Why don't you help yourself to a glass of orange juice, young man? Your mama and me—we got some catching up to do.'

Satisfied that there was nothing unusual in this request, Dominic skipped across to the tray. Balancing the jug of fruit juice with two hands, he made a creditable attempt to pour some into a perspex glass, his concentration centred on this task to the exclusion of all else.

'I guess Miss Julie told you what happened,' Melinda continued, lowering her voice, and Abby nodded. 'But she didn't tell Mr Jake about you, did she?'

'No.' Abby squeezed the water out of her hair, and shook her head.

'No.' Melinda shifted her ample weight from one foot to the other. 'I thought not.'

'Why?' Abby hesitated. 'You think I did the wrong thing by coming here?'

'Heck, no. I didn't say that.' Melinda put one hand on her hip. 'I know you'd be wanting to see young Dominic. Ain't nothing wrong with that. How could there be?'

Abby frowned. Melinda sometimes had a curious way of coming to the point. 'But—you're concerned about something?'

Melinda turned to give Dominic a wide smile, and then sighed. 'I just hope you know what you're doing, that's all,' she admitted softly. 'Mr Jake ain't in no state to fight over the boy.'

Abby put the towel aside, and regarded the old woman thoughtfully. 'How sick is he, Melinda?' she asked, waiting with some apprehension for the answer.

Melinda shrugged. 'Well, he ain't well, that's for sure.'

'Do—do you think it's serious?'

'I think it could be.' Melinda paused. 'Ain't nothing else in his life but Dominic, and that old company of his. And, Lord knows, that young man there ain't old enough to take that burden off his shoulders!'

Abby made a helpless gesture. 'But—what can I do?'

'That ain't for me to say.'

'Oh, Melinda!'

'Well—you could try and get him to take things easier,' she said at last.

'Me?'

'Ain't no one else,' she remarked, much as Julie had done earlier that morning. 'I guess you got no choice.'

CHAPTER FOUR

LUNCH was served in the air-conditioned luxury of a small dining-room. At this time of the year, it was not a meal that could comfortably be enjoyed out of doors. The noonday heat, and the humidity, made dining al fresco inadvisable and, besides, Abby knew she had had enough of the sun for one day.

Although she had showered and changed into a silk vest and the shorts she had been wearing earlier, she was unhappily aware that her shoulders were prickling already. Despite her efforts to protect her skin, the ultra-violet light must have penetrated the water of the pool, and standing talking to Melinda afterwards had only added to the problem.

Of course, she reflected, as she smoothed a light moisturising cream over her cheekbones, in other circumstances she wouldn't have cared. The warmth of the sun on their skin was something most people came to these islands for. But, there again, she was not most people, and if she wanted to fulfil her contract she would have to be more careful in future.

If! The realisation of what she had been thinking was almost shocking. There was no 'if' about it. The contract she had with Marcia was not negotiable. She had one week's freedom, and that was all.

There were only two places laid at the round ebony table. Only two scarlet raffia place mats; only two sets of silver cutlery. At first, Abby thought Dominic must be having his lunch elsewhere. But, just as she was on the point of asking Rosa why her son wasn't joining them, Dominic appeared.

Like her, he had changed, and his hair was neatly combed. Evidently Melinda, who had insisted on taking charge of the boy while Abby went to take her shower, had helped him freshen up, for now his shorts and shirt were neatly buttoned and he smelled healthily of soap.

However, like hers, his eyes went first of all to the table, and he frowned. 'Where's Daddy? Isn't he having his lunch with us?'

'It seems not.' Abby turned as Rosa entered the room behind them, carrying a huge platter of cooked meats and salad. 'Is—is Dominic's father eating in his study?'

Rosa set the platter down on the table before replying. Then, folding her hands over her ample stomach, she said, 'Mr Jake don't want no lunch, Miz Abby. He says he's not hungry.'

Abby sighed. 'But that doesn't sound very—sensible,' she murmured, not wanting to alarm Dominic, and Rosa arched her dark brows in agreement. 'Um—where is he? Surely he's not still working!'

'No, ma'am.' Rosa gave Dominic a wary look, and then added, 'He's—um—resting, Miz Abby. He said to tell the little one he'd see him later.'

'Resting?' Abby mouthed the words inaudibly, and Rosa nodded.

'That's right,' she agreed, jerking a surreptitious thumb towards the ceiling. 'You know what I mean?'

She meant Jake had gone back to bed, and Abby was concerned. She guessed Rosa was concerned, too, but didn't like to say so in front of the boy. It was an impossible situation.

'So—why don't you have some lunch?' Rosa suggested now, drawing Dominic's attention to the table. 'Look, I've made you some of those cheese puffs you're so fond of. Perhaps your mama would like to try one, too. I'm sure she's just dying for you to ask her.'

'Are you, Mummy?'

Dominic was easily diverted, and Abby made a determined effort to pay attention to what her son was saying. 'What? Oh—yes. They look delicious!' she agreed, bending down beside him. 'But, you know, I've got to watch what I eat. Too many cheese puffs and I'll turn into a butter ball!'

'I'd say you had a long way to go before that happened,' observed Rosa drily. And then, in an undertone, 'You two have lunch. Young Dominic has a rest himself after. If you want to know if Mr Jake is all right, perhaps you ought to find out then.'

Abby stared at the housekeeper blankly. *'Me!'* she wanted to say, but the word dried in her throat. Yet how could she take it upon herself to check up on Jake? She was reluctant to do it, and he sure as hell wouldn't welcome her interference.

All the same, she couldn't entirely dismiss the responsibility. As she sat alone at the lunch table, lingering over her second cup of coffee, she had to admit it seemed to be expected of her. Even Melinda, who had come to collect Dominic and take him, albeit protesting, for his rest, obviously assumed that she had no alternative.

And why not? she asked herself ruefully. She had come here, after all. She had wasted no time in booking her passage to the island. But, to see *Dominic*, she reminded herself impatiently. Not to get involved with the man she'd grown to hate.

The house was very quiet as Abby made her way upstairs. Dust motes hung in every shaft of sunlight, and the air-conditioning was just a barely audible hum. Beneath her feet, the treads of the stairs were shiny and cool, and she curled her toes appreciatively. She had left her canvas shoes beside the pool, and it was pleasurably familiar to go barefoot.

Jake's rooms opened off the galleried landing. The double doors to his sitting-room confronted her at the head of the stairs, and she knew from past experience that his bedroom was beyond. It was possible to enter the bedroom by means of the dressing-room, which also opened on to the landing, but that entrance was too personal. If she had to do this, and she was still not convinced of its advisability, she would rather knock at the door of the sitting-room. That way, at least, he could not accuse her of invading his privacy.

But when she knocked on one of the white panelled doors of the sitting-room, there was no reply. Even when she balled her knuckles and hammered quite noisily against the wood, there was no response. If Jake was inside he was either deaf or unconscious, she decided bitterly. Or *dead*, an inner voice taunted, and without any more hesitation she sought the round brass handle.

The room beyond the double doors was much more opulent than she remembered. A seductively soft carpet, cushioned chairs and sofas in tapestries and velvets, and trailing fronds of greenery spilling from porcelain jardinières. The walls were hung with silk, and there were several exotic paintings, and the room more resembled a boudoir than the comfortable parlour it used to be.

Eve? wondered Abby tautly, trying to ignore the more obvious connotations of this conclusion as she marched across the room to the bedroom door. Surely Jake was not responsible for such—bad taste? Even she, with her doubtful background, would not have chosen to decorate a room in such a way.

Still, at least her indignation enabled her to open the bedroom door with more confidence. For a moment, she was filled with the injustice of what she had just seen, and her apprehension was in abeyance. But, although her hand shook a little as she pushed the door inward, her trepidation proved groundless. Like the sitting-room before it, the bedroom was empty, the air in the apartment faintly musty and damp.

'Were you looking for me?'

Abby nearly jumped out of her skin at the unexpected voice behind her. Although she had been all keyed up when she'd entered the suite of rooms, events since had relaxed her defences, and the last thing she had expected was for Jake to appear. Swinging round, she leant weakly against the door-frame, summoning all her composure to withstand his cool appraisal. Even the fact that he was wearing a towelling bathrobe and little else was no compensation. For the moment she was shocked and defenceless, and hardly able to offer an explanation.

Jake's mouth tightened. 'I asked if you were looking for me,' he repeated. 'Or were you just curious? Well, I'm sorry to disappoint you, but I don't use these rooms any more.'

Abby swallowed. 'How—how did you know where I was?'

'Are you kidding?' Jake stared at her disbelievingly. 'I should think the population of Laguna Cay knows where you are!'

Abby pressed her lips together. 'You heard me knocking?'

'I heard you,' Jake agreed drily. 'What were you trying to do? Wake the dead?'

His words were so close to what Abby had been thinking earlier that for a moment she couldn't respond. And Jake groaned.

'Oh, no,' he said wearily. 'You didn't really think there was something wrong, did you? My God, I was only taking a siesta. Believe it or not, lots of people on these islands do the same.'

Abby straightened away from the door. 'Not without lunch,' she said, with more certainty. 'I—was worried about you. I came to see if you were all right.'

Jake regarded her broodingly for a long moment, and then he dropped his gaze. 'Well, as you can see, I am,' he remarked, turning back towards the door. 'I—thank you for your concern, but it really wasn't necessary.'

'Wasn't it?' Abby followed him out on to the landing and closed the doors behind her. She allowed her eyes to move over his pale face with more intensity. 'Why didn't you have any lunch? Was it—was it because I was there?'

'No!'

Jake's response was impatient now, and, raising his hand in what might have been a gesture of farewell, he walked away along the corridor that led in the opposite direction to Abby's own room. Clearly he considered the matter settled, but Abby was still doubtful and, taking a deep breath, she set off after him.

Jake turned halfway along the corridor and saw her following him, and he scowled. 'This is not the way to your room,' he said pointedly, tightening the belt of his bathrobe. But Abby was not perturbed.

'I know it's not,' she said. 'But don't you think I ought to know where you sleep? After all, I might need you unexpectedly and not know where to find you. In the night, for example, when everyone else is asleep.'

'You won't be here long enough for that to be a problem,' retorted Jake bleakly, evidently assuming the harshness of his response to be a sufficient deterrent. Without waiting to see how she reacted to it, he inclined his head and continued on his way, only discovering Abby was still behind him when he reached the door to his apartments.

'Look, are you trying to annoy me?' he demanded as she came up to him, but Abby refused to be deflected. She was still not convinced of his reasons for avoiding lunch, and besides, she was curious to know which rooms he now occupied.

So, instead of pausing in the doorway as he had done, she stepped past him into the room, ignoring his startled intake of breath as she gazed with interest around the room.

Unlike the rooms which she and Jake had once shared, and which were now so grossly over-furnished, this room was not dissimilar to her own. Actually, it was smaller, the sitting area separated from the bedroom by only a curved arch decorated with wrought-iron mouldings. In the sitting-room there was only a table, near the window, with a couple of fan-backed woven chairs, and an arm-chair with a book upturned on its seat. And the bedroom was similarly functional, with a fruitwood chest of drawers, and a pair of matching tables beside the bed. The bed itself was rather more than functional, she admitted, noticing that it had recently been occupied. She doubted it would even fit into her bedroom at her apartment in London, but in these surroundings it did not look out of place.

However, her gaze only skimmed over these observations. Curiosity was one thing; voyeurism was another. She had no wish to know who shared Jake's bed, she told herself. Not now; not ever.

'Will you get out of here?'

Jake was standing just inside the door, but it was still wide open, and it was obvious he had no intention of closing it. Abby almost smiled. The unlikely thought crossed her mind that Jake wasn't altogether sure how to handle this situation, that she briefly held an advantage, if she could only figure out what to do with it.

'We need to talk,' she said at last, casting an innocent glance in his direction before walking towards the sheer muslin curtains billowing at the open doors to the balcony. Pulling the vest out of the waistband of her shorts, she moved it like a fan against her midriff. 'Mmm—isn't it hot? But isn't this view terrific?'

The door slammed shut behind her, but as Jake hadn't moved she couldn't be sure whether he had pushed it or the breeze from the open window had accomplished the feat. In any event, they were alone in Jake's bedroom, and Abby couldn't help the treacherous memories of other afternoons, exactly like this . . .

'What makes you think I won't have you thrown off the island—again?' demanded Jake harshly, but there was a pinched look about his lips now, and his eyes moved towards the bed almost desperately. He ought not to be out of bed at all, thought Abby uneasily, torn between the urge to take advantage of his weakness and the equally strong desire not to exacerbate his condition.

'I think we should suspend our differences for the time being,' she declared, moving away from the window to run a questing finger over the brass rail at the foot of the bed. 'I'm here now, and there's not a lot you can do about it—without upsetting Dominic, I mean.' She paused. 'And yourself.'

Jake uttered a frustrated sound. 'I've told you,' he snarled. 'I'm not an invalid! I realise you'd like me to be, because it would make it that much easier for you. But, I'm sorry to disappoint you, I'm still in full possession of my faculties! And I know why you really came here. I guess you couldn't wait to jump on a plane when Julie told you I was in the hospital. You thought it was an ideal opportunity to get at Dominic, while I wasn't around to stop you. What did you plan to do, Abby? Take him back to England and start immediate custody proceedings?' He shook his head. 'It doesn't occur to you that he might be happy here, does it? You have this sick notion that a child—that a child belongs with its mother, no matter how—how undesirable that mother might be, and nothing—nothing's—nothing's going—to—shift . . .'

By this time, Jake was gasping for breath, and the spontaneous anger his words had provoked was instantly dispelled. Whatever Jake said, he *was* ill, and Abby's first instincts were protective.

Ignoring his agitated gestures for her to leave him alone, she took his arm and urged him firmly towards the bed. Then, pressing him down on to the mattress, she bent and unfastened the cord of his dressing-gown, sliding the towelling robe off his shoulders and easing him back against the pillows. She was momentarily disconcerted by the realisation that he was naked beneath the robe, and for once her determined assertion that she had no feeling for Jake whatsoever was put to the test. It was almost impossible for her to maintain a sense of detachment, when this man's body had once been as familiar to her as her own. She was aware that her hands were trembling as she drew the bathrobe away, and she quickly pulled the covers over him before he noticed her distraction.

Still, it was impossible not to show her concern about him, and after assuring herself that his colour did seem a little better she located the bathroom and went to get him a glass of water. Turning on the tap until the water ran cool, she was forced to look at her reflection in the mirror above the basin. Her eyes were bright, and her cheeks were pink, and there was a definite trace of a quiver about her mouth. Oh, God, she thought, what was she letting herself in for?

By the time she returned to the bedroom, Jake had almost recovered from the attack. He lay against his pillows, watching her with haggard eyes as she came round the bed towards him. It was obvious these attacks robbed him of what little strength he had, and she was overwhelmed with sympathy.

Aware of his frustration with his condition, she nevertheless seated herself on the edge of the bed beside him and held the glass of water to his lips.

'I can do that,' he muttered hoarsely, taking the glass from her and managing to swallow a few sips. 'God, what a bloody situation! Why can't those—doctors find me a cure? God knows, I pay them enough!'

The word he used before 'doctors' was not one Abby would have cared to repeat, but she sensed his humiliation. He hated feeling helpless. It was not a circumstance he was familiar with .

Putting out her hand, she stroked her thumb across his· forehead, feeling the beads of perspiration, cool against her skin. Although he flinched, there was not a lot he could do to stop her, and she drew her hand away again and tucked her thumb between her lips. It was almost an involuntary action. Not until she tasted the slightly salt tang on her tongue did she realise what she had done. But then it was too late to regret it, and her eyes meeting Jake's were just the tiniest bit defensive.

'You know,' she said, after a moment, needing to dispel the sudden intimacy between them, 'the cure's in your own hands. You've been told to rest and take things easy. And instead, you're behaving as if there's never been anything wrong.'

'Am I?' Jake heaved a deep breath, and shifted restlessly against the pillows. Evidently, he was feeling better, and when he raised his hand to rake his fingers through his hair it was all Abby could do to remain where she was. With the covers slipping to his waist, the moist hair on his chest and in the hollow beneath his arm was disturbingly attractive, and it would have been oh, so easy to touch his damp skin.

'Tell me,' he said suddenly, fixing her with an intent gaze, 'why are you being so nice to me?'

Abby caught her breath. 'Am I being nice?'

'You know you are.' Jake took another deep breath, and regarded her curiously. 'In the circumstances, I'd have expected you to be pleased that I'm such an obvious wreck! Instead of which, you bring me water, and—to misquote Congreve—soothe my savage breast. Why?'

Abby took the glass out of his hand, and set it carefully on the table beside the bed. Then, lifting her slim shoulders in a gesture of indifference, she said, 'I'm not a sadist. Whatever you think, I don't like seeing people suffer.'

'Not even me?' he persisted grimly, and Abby dragged her eyes away from his to assume a contemplation of the coverlet.

'Not even you,' she conceded, making a play of straightening the sheet over the gold silk bedspread, and then gasped in surprise when his hands closed over hers.

'Don't do that,' he said, causing her startled gaze to seek his. 'I'm not your responsibility. If I choose to go to hell my own way, then you don't have to get involved.'

'But I am involved,' said Abby, releasing herself without too much effort, although she could still feel the hardness of Jake's lean fingers around her knuckles. 'You forget—I'm Dominic's mother. Whatever concerns him, concerns me.'

Jake's jaw tightened. 'I don't forget anything,' he muttered, but the effort of making his point seemed to have tired him again. 'Oh, God—if only I didn't feel so weak! If only there were some pill I could take that would miraculously give me strength.'

'Well, there isn't,' said Abby flatly, ignoring his protest not to touch him, and stroking the strands of damp dark hair back from his hot forehead. 'For once, you're going to have to do as you're told, like it or not.'

Jake swore. 'Like hell!'

'Well, what's your alternative?' Abby murmured wryly. 'Do you want to kill yourself?'

'I won't kill myself!'

'I wouldn't guarantee that, if I were you.' Abby couldn't deny a *frisson* of dismay at these words, but she had to say something to convince him. She hesitated. 'And what do you think would happen to Dominic then?'

Jake made no response to this deliberate piece of provocation, and Abby sighed. 'Well,' she said defensively, 'can't you think of anything to say? Like—bitch, for instance. Or some other complimentary epithet. I seem to remember you knew them all. And used them.'

Jake still said nothing, and, as the silence between them stretched, Abby decided she might as well abandon any further attempt to get him to see sense for the moment. Jake wasn't going to listen to her. He never had. Not about anything.

But when she would have got to her feet he caught her wrist between his fingers and kept her where she was. 'All right,' he said, his golden eyes holding her unwilling gaze. 'Suppose I accept that what you say is—partly true. That there is no magic cure for what's wrong with me. That rest—and relaxation—are the only things that are going to help. If I agree to the prognosis, will you leave here?'

Abby swallowed. 'When?'

Jake's mouth tightened. 'Is today too soon?'

Abby caught her breath. 'You beast!'

'Why?' Jake's fingers dug into her soft flesh. 'Because I'm not sick enough not to see what you're trying to do? You know you'll never succeed in persuading me to let you stay here by fair means, so you're prepared to play dirty. Like pretending you care what happens to me, for example!'

But she *did* care! Insidiously, the thought came to her. Staring at him through eyes made hot and gritty by unshed tears, Abby was forced to acknowledge what she had been fighting ever since she came to the island. She did care. And, like it or not, he could still hurt her.

'Cat got your tongue?' Jake taunted, and, although all her instincts were telling her to get away from him now, at once, some stronger intuition kept her where she was. It would be too easy for him if she walked out of here. Too easy if she let him goad her into some impulsive reaction to his callous show of indifference. Was he indifferent? Or was he as aware as she was of what there had once been between them?

'I—I was just wondering why you're so—afraid that I might stay,' she ventured at last, deciding she had nothing to lose. He had already threatened to have her thrown off the island—again. And this might be her last chance to find out how he really felt, however painful that might be.

'Afraid?' Jake echoed now, releasing her wrist as if it had suddenly burned him. 'Are you crazy?'

'I don't think so.' Abby was having a problem keeping her breathing even, but at least the adrenalin pumping through her veins had banished the betraying sting of tears. 'You're certainly eager to get rid of me. I just wondered why, that's all. What harm am I doing here? Don't you think I deserve to spend some time with my son?'

Jake glared at her. 'What do you really want from me, Abby?' he demanded. 'Are you short of money, is that it? Did you come here hoping I'd be willing to pay to get rid of you? Well, let me remind you, you were the one who refused to accept any financial help from me. As I recall it, I had my solicitor draw up a contract——'

'I don't want your money!' Just for a moment, Abby's composure slipped, and she was in imminent danger of undoing all the good she had done. But then the realisation that he was trying to turn this conversation to his own ends by baiting her surfaced, and a smile tugged at her lips as she met his furious stare.

'Then what do you want?' he snapped, levering himself up on his elbows. 'For heaven's sake, Abby, state your price!'

'Perhaps—perhaps I just want—you,' she murmured, realising instinctively just what she had to do. Ignoring the look of disbelief that crossed his face, she laid her palms against his cheeks. Then, before he had a chance to drag himself free, she bent and put her lips to his, rubbing her tongue against his mouth with sensuous persistence.

Jake collapsed against his pillows almost involuntarily. Abby guessed it was the shock of what she was doing as much as any inherent weakness, but it did free his hands to try and push her away. But Abby wouldn't let him. Whatever idea she had had when she first touched his lips with hers had been quickly superseded by the sheer delight of feeling Jake's mouth moving beneath her tongue. It was a totally new experience for her to initiate their lovemaking, and despite his protestations she knew Jake was weakening. She thought he would have liked to utter his objections; indeed, she was pretty sure he would have done so, if when he parted his lips her tongue had not slid into his mouth. But it did, and the wave of heat that engulfed her was not wholly self-induced.

His hands, which had risen to grasp her upper arms and force some space between them, were suddenly gripping her flesh with unexpected strength, and through the fine material of her vest she could feel the taut muscles of his torso. She was resting on him now, her breasts crushed against his chest, and the thin layer of silk was all that was between them. But even that was an obstruction, and she was not surprised when he pushed the cloth above her breasts and she felt his heated skin against her own.

And all the while her mouth was clinging to his, so that now she was finding trouble with her breathing. What had begun as an exercise on her part to prove Jake was not indifferent to her had turned into a hungry satiation of the senses, and she was no longer in control, merely an eager participant.

She would have drawn back then, but she couldn't. Jake's hand was at her nape, under the silky moistness of her hair, fusing her mouth to his with ever-increasing urgency. His other hand was pressed against the side of her breast, his thumb finding the tight nipple that surged against his skin. There was no part of her being that was not responding to the wild excitement he was now generating, and when he kicked the sheets aside and rolled her over on to her back her arms went around his neck almost automatically.

Her body was exposed to him now, and he took full advantage of the fact. The constricting band of her vest was quickly tossed aside, and her breasts swelled and hardened beneath his gaze. Jake's eyes when he looked at her were dark, and glazed with passion, and if he hated her for what she had done here he was not inclined to discuss it at present. On the contrary, like hers, his skin was hot and slick with sweat, and it wasn't the warmth of the air-conditioned room that was responsible. They were both consumed by the fire they had created, and for the moment that was all that mattered. Jake didn't look pale now, Abby noticed unsteadily. His eyes were glittering, and his face was flushed with his emotions. She didn't know what he was thinking as he filled his hands with her soft flesh, but his mouth was wholly sensual as he suckled at her breasts.

Moisture flooded Abby's body as she felt the erotic tugging at her nipple, and her hand slid over his shoulders, and down his back, spreading sensuously over his narrow hips. His buttocks pushed against her palms as he ground his thighs against her, the rigid strength of his arousal nudging her legs apart.

And she wanted to part her legs. The ache that throbbed inside her could only be eased by the swollen penetration of his body, and her hands went naturally to the waistband of her shorts. She wanted to ease them down, over her hips, kick them aside, and let Jake touch the dewy core of her womanhood. She wanted—oh, she wanted him inside her, filling her as only he could, her legs around him as he thrust ever more urgently into her body. . .

She was so aroused by now that she could hardly think straight any more. Jake was kissing her, and caressing her, his tongue seeking out the sensitive curve of her hip, the scented heart of her navel. Pretty soon, he'd push her shorts off for her, and then—and then——

The sound of Dominic's voice in the courtyard outside brought her abruptly to her senses. Dear God, she thought faintly, what was she doing? What was she letting Jake do? In a few minutes, it would be too late, and she was not prepared for this. It was so long since she had had to take those kind of precautions, and the idea of going to see a doctor before making this trip had been plainly ridiculous. In consequence, she could be running the risk of another—in this case *unwanted* pregnancy. It had only taken one lapse on her part for Dominic to become a reality. But she had wanted Jake's baby then, more than anything else in the world.

But not now, she told herself fiercely, forcing the sensuous waves of submission aside. She could not afford to make any more mistakes. Not when she was no longer Jake's lover, only a substitute for his frustrated libido.

She waited until Jake lifted his weight to move over her again, and then rolled swiftly sidewards. She made it, because she was nearer the edge than she had anticipated, and tumbled off the bed. She landed on her knees on the floor, feeling totally sick and humiliated, in her cotton shorts and little else. Her canvas shoes had been discarded earlier, and she scrambled desperately for her vest for some protection. So much for her efforts to maintain the upper hand, she thought bitterly, tugging it over her head. All she had succeeded in doing was creating a need she dared not satisfy.

When she got unsteadily to her feet, some distance away from the bed to prevent Jake from grabbing her, she found him lying on his back, watching her with curiously guarded eyes. She had expected anger, violence even, certainly contempt, but there was nothing she could identify. Instead, she was the one who had to practically drag her eyes away from his nude body, aware that, however thin he might be, he was still the sexiest man she had ever seen.

'You're going, then,' he said, making no attempt to cover himself, and Abby took a breath before nodding.

'Dominic's outside,' she said, as if that was a reason. 'Um—he'll be wondering where I am.'

Jake inclined his head. Curiously enough, he looked better somehow, more at ease, though she could tell from the dominant state of his sex that he was anything but relaxed.

'OK,' he said, folding his arms beneath his head, and regarding her with cool appraisal. 'Don't let me keep you.'

'I won't.'

Abby felt compelled to make the sharp retort, but as she let herself out of the bedroom she was helplessly confounded. She would have sworn that Jake would take his frustration out on her. But instead, he had left her in a total state of confusion.

CHAPTER FIVE

ABBY spent the rest of the day at the mercy of her nerves. That scene with Jake in his bedroom had left her in a highly emotional frame of mind, and it was all she could do not to snap at Dominic when he took advantage of her distraction. She tried to put what had happened behind her, and behave normally, but it wasn't easy even to pretend. Dominic was so like his father, in so many ways, that everything he did was an innocent reminder, a cause to make Abby bite her tongue.

She knew what was wrong with her, of course. She had seen too many neurotic females not to know what happened when a woman was sexually frustrated. She was on edge, and irritable; her skin felt taut, and overly sensitive; and she was half tearful at the realisation that she had no way of assuaging her tension.

It was a new experience for her. Until she and Jake had begun to live together, she had never regarded sex as an important factor of her existence. Indeed, it was something she had preferred to live without, and she'd been firmly convinced she didn't need it.

But then, she had never known how it could be between a man and a woman until Jake had entered her life, so that was hardly surprising. Her experiences of sex had been brief and sordid, and she had never imagined it could be such a beautiful thing.

Not that Jake had believed that, she reflected bitterly later that evening, after Dominic was tucked safely in bed. As she applied a cooling moisturiser to her shoulders, she was forced to acknowledge that Max had had the most lasting influence on her life. Although she

74

had loved Jake desperately, he had not loved her enough, and, though she might despise Max for his methods of getting even, there was no denying that his emotions had been superior to Jake's.

But what emotions? she pondered, unable to prevent the shiver of apprehension that slid down her spine at the remembrance. It was certainly not love that had guided Max's hand. How jealous he must have been of her happiness to destroy her life so completely!

Her fingers, massaging her burning skin, increased their pressure with painful consequences, and she let out a cry. But whether her cry was wholly the result of a physical reaction she could not be absolutely sure. But what was apparent, as she endeavoured to spread the cream more gently, was her own inability to control her thoughts. Although it was a long time since she had allowed herself to think about Max, in the present situation it was difficult not to, impossible not to speculate how things might have been.

Abby was only sixteen when she first met Max Cervantes. At that time, she was working behind the reception desk of one of the larger hotels at Heathrow, checking guests in and out, and answering phones when necessary. It was not a bad job. Indeed, when she was first offered the position, and the option of sharing a room in a nearby hostel with one of the other girls, she had practically jumped at the chance. But six months of answering enquiries and tearing off computer printouts had taken the shine off it somewhat, and she was ripe for seduction when Max made his suggestion.

Not that she had recognised his intentions at that time. On the contrary, she had still been naïve enough to imagine that there were honest benefactors in the world, and Max's approach had allayed any fears she might have had.

Up until that time, her life had not been easy, but she had never been the type to complain. Orphaned at the age of six, with no close relations willing to take the responsibility for her upbringing, she had spent the last ten years in a children's home. Without any real academic skills, she had left the Ealing comprehensive school with only average grades in most subjects, the only exception being languages, in which she had excelled. That was how she had managed to get the job at the Heathrow Monleigh; that, and a pleasant, outgoing personality, which she had always believed covered a multitude of sins.

She had never considered herself particularly attractive. Achieving her present height by the age of twelve had let her in for all manner of jokes and teasing. And it was true, she had looked like a beanpole at that age. With toffee-brown hair, and eyes that were more grey than blue, she had considered her appearance as uninspiring as the majority of her examination results, and in consequence she was totally overwhelmed when Max told her she had the makings of a good model.

Of course, she thought at first that he was teasing. As a business traveller, Max had been often in and out of the hotel on his way to Europe, or Australia, or more frequently the United States. Although he had told her he lived in London, he usually spent the night before a flight at the hotel, and Abby had got accustomed to seeing him checking in and checking out. He usually looked for her to deal with his account, and she had begun to regard him as a friend. He always asked how she was, and what she was doing, and, although fraternising with the guests was not encouraged, Max always arranged it so that none of the supervisors was in attendance when he approached the desk. Besides which, he was *old*. Forty-five or fifty, at least. Abby was convinced his interest in her was perfectly innocent. He must know that as he was several inches shorter than she was, with thinning hair and a slight paunch, he was not likely to appeal to her. In any case, why would a man of his wealth and experience be interested in a sixteen-year-old receptionist? There were plenty of beautiful older women in the hotel. He probably felt sorry for her, and was trying to be kind.

However, his comments about her appearance came as a complete surprise. Although she knew she had put on weight in recent years, and that her figure was now passably presentable, she still regarded herself as something of a freak. None of the other girls she worked with was as tall as she was, and she had grown accustomed to wearing conservative colours and low heels in an effort not to draw attention to her height.

Until Max made his startling observation, she had known little about his background. She had assumed he was a financier, or an expert in micro-technology. She had never imagined he might be involved in the fashion industry. But then, why should she? She was only sixteen, after all, and she rarely looked at fashion magazines.

But one of the other girls, who had overheard their conversation, put her straight. 'Don't you know who that is?' she exclaimed impatiently. 'That's Max Cervantes! *The* Max Cervantes. My God, don't you know anything? Where have you been for the last ten years?'

'I know who he is,' Abby mumbled defensively. 'I've dealt with him often enough. He—he's frequently in and out of the hotel. He's just come back from Singapore.'

'But you don't know why he went to Singapore, do you?' the other girl taunted, and Abby got the impression that she was half angry with her for being so ignorant. 'For heaven's sake, his agency's been filming a fashion spread for next year's spring collections. Max Cervantes' agency rivals any in his field.'

Abby remembered how she had felt at that moment. Her mouth had gone dry, and she had stared at the other girl, half unbelieving. 'He runs a photographic agency?' she asked, and her companion sighed.

'Not runs, *owns*,' she replied. 'Didn't I just say so?'

'Then—then you think he wasn't—joking, when he said—what he said.'

'I doubt it.' The other girl was terse. 'Not that I'd like to get involved with a man like him,' she added, almost defensively now. 'He does have quite a reputation. I'd watch my step, if I were you. Unless you really feel you could cut it.'

Her deliberate use of the slang terminology was meant to remind Abby that she, at least, was unimpressed by what had happened, but Abby wondered. If he was serious, and he did have some intention of offering to help her, ought she to accept it? After all, the opportunity to become a fashion model was one of those once-in-a-lifetime chances that seldom came your way, and if she turned it down wouldn't she always wonder how successful she might have been?

Of course, after sleeping on it, she was less optimistic about the whole thing. Just because Max Cervantes had said that she had the makings of a good model, there was no reason to assume that he intended to take a hand in her affairs. She had blown a perfectly innocent remark out of all proportion, and, had the other receptionist not spoken to her about it, she would probably have forgotten it by now.

But she didn't forget it, even though it was another three weeks before she saw Max again. During that time, she alternated between moods of high excitement—when the idea of giving up her job at the hotel and travelling all over the world on different assignments, as Max Cervantes did, filled her with elation—and more practical days, when she was forced to acknowledge that she was not experienced enough to consider such a choice. What if the other girl had been right? What if Max Cervantes was interested in her body, in more than one way? In those circumstances, she was certain she would refuse to have anything to do with him. The very idea of going to bed with someone old enough to be her father was repulsive. She simply wasn't the kind of girl to sell herself, whatever the incentive.

Max's next visit to the hotel coincided with one of Abby's afternoons off. The girls on the reception desk worked split shifts every third week, which meant Abby was free every afternoon from twelve to six. She was walking across the car park, on her way to catch the bus which would take her into Egham, when Max stepped out of his car and hailed her.

Afterwards, she did wonder if he had been waiting for her to come out of the hotel. He could easily have found out what shift she was on and intercepted her. Whatever, her excitement at seeing him again far outweighed her caution, and she didn't hesitate before she walked towards him.

'You're not leaving,' he said, and she quickly explained her hours of working.

'You'll have to get someone else to look after you today, Mr Cervantes,' she declared ruefully. 'I've got some shopping to do, and I won't be back until this evening.'

'Then perhaps I ought to delay checking in until later,' he remarked, his swarthy face mirroring his humour. Although he spoke English without an accent, Abby guessed he was of Spanish extraction, and she wondered if his Latin blood inspired his artistic temperament.

During the past weeks, she had taken the opportunity to study several magazines that dealt with clothes and fashion, and some amateur investigation had enlightened her as to which models worked for which agency. It was impossible for her to be objective, of course. For one thing, she didn't honestly know what she was looking for. But one thing was apparent: the advertisements that featured Cervantes' models were all tasteful and elegant, and aesthetically beautiful, the backgrounds simple, but imaginative, the clothes expensive.

Abby didn't know how to respond now. She wasn't sure whether he was joking with her or not. She was sure he must be, but then, why had he attracted her attention?

She was searching madly for something to say that would not sound too inane when he invited her to have lunch with him. 'Oh—not here,' he appended swiftly, noticing the awkward glance she cast over her shoulder. 'There's a place I know, just outside Windsor. It's not far, and I'd really like to talk to you.'

Abby's hesitation was barely discernible. Why not? she argued with the voice inside her that warned her to be careful. It was only lunch, after all. A man like Max Cervantes was hardly likely to abduct her. Or was he? How did she really know?

'You can tell your mother where you're going,' he inserted suddenly, as if sensing her hesitation, but Abby shook her head.

'It's all right,' she said swiftly, not yet prepared to admit that she didn't have a mother to tell. 'Thank you, I'd like to have lunch with you. Although I really can't imagine why you want to talk to me.'

'Can't you?' Max's eyes narrowed, and, feeling the colour rise in her cheeks, she wondered if he was a mind-reader as well. 'Oh, Abby, I'm sure you can guess exactly what I want to talk to you about. I've thought about you a lot these past few weeks and I know, if you'll let me, I can do a great deal to help you. But I don't propose to conduct a business discussion here, in the car park. So—get into the car. Isn't it fortunate I didn't have time to dismiss Harry before I saw you?'

The burly Scotsman, who was introduced as Max's chauffeur, opened the car door for her, and Abby squashed any lingering doubts and stepped inside. How many girls were given this kind of an opportunity? she wondered. And how many girls would refuse to take the chance, if it were offered to them?

Her fears were totally allayed during the lunch that followed. Sitting in the kind of restaurant she had hitherto only seen on television, she was offered caviare and smoked salmon, fillet steak with a puff-pastry shell, and freshly picked strawberries, with a topping of Cornish cream. She refused to drink any of the wine that flowed equally as freely, but she did accept a virgin cocktail, after Max had explained that it contained no alcohol. And, sipping her drink, she allowed her eyes to wander round the other tables, and the sometimes famous faces she saw there. Until now, she hadn't really believed that people actually took all this for granted. Somehow she had always imagined that television pictures had to be larger than life. Well, the stories maybe, she acknowledged, but not their settings.

It was not until after their coffee had been served that Max got down to the real purpose of this outing. Then, with the minimum amount of fuss, he explained that he thought Abby had what it took to become a successful model. That if she was willing he was prepared to invest a great deal of money in her future.

'Because you're a natural,' he replied, when she asked him why in a quavering voice. 'You're tall; you've got good bone-structure; you move well. And you're young, which means you can learn.'

Abby stared at him. For so long now she had regarded herself as a misfit, and to be told that the characteristics about herself she least liked were the ones he admired was unbelievable.

'You don't believe me.' Max's voice was flat now, and Abby swallowed.

'I—don't know,' she admitted awkwardly. 'It just seems so—so incredible.'

'Everyone has to start somewhere,' remarked Max drily, taking a mouthful of the liqueur he had ordered to accompany his coffee. 'And it's not a wholly altruistic gesture.'

'It's not?' Abby was wary.

'No.' He was faintly impatient now. 'I'm not a philanthropist, Abby. I'm a businessman, and this is a business deal I'm offering you. I expect to make a great deal of money out of your success.'

Abby took a deep breath. 'You wouldn't—that is—you don't...'

'Fancy you?' His eyes narrowed above his pouched cheeks, and just for a moment she felt a chill. 'My dear Abby, if I were to—start a relationship with every model on my books, I'd have very little energy left for anything else. Do I make myself clear?'

Abby flushed. 'Perfectly.'

'Good.'

He was summoning the waiter as he spoke, and Abby knew this was her last chance to accept his offer. If she refused him now, she would never get a second chance, and she wanted to accept. Oh, God! She wanted to accept...

A year later, Abby was able to laugh at her fears. The past months had changed her from a nervous schoolgirl into a confident young woman, and so many wonderful things had happened to her that she had had no time to worry about the future.

And Max had been kind, *so kind* to her. Within weeks of her accepting his offer he had arranged for her to leave the hostel and move into a comfortable apartment with two of his other models, and for the first time in her life Abby had had a room of her own. The other girls had accepted her without question, and if they didn't regard Max as quite the benefactor she did that was probably because their backgrounds were so very different from her own.

In any event, they were friendly, and Abby was glad of their support. Although the idea of putting on pretty clothes and posing before a photographer sounded easy, it proved to be the hardest thing she had ever done, and there were evenings, when she got back to the flat, when she wondered why she had ever thought she could do it.

But time went on, and she became more assured, not only of her ability, but of her appearance. Gone were the days when she had tried to minimise her height. Now, mixing with the other models, many of whom were six feet tall or more, she slipped her feet into heels with growing confidence. She no longer regarded herself as being too slim. On the contrary, her increase in salary meant she had to guard against buying too much rich food, and she learned to eat a balanced diet and watch her weight.

There were many compensations, of course. The lessons she learned about her hair and make-up taught her to appreciate the importance of style and colouring. She quickly realised how amateurish her own attempts at making up her face had been, when applying a cream-based foundation and lipstick had seemed all that was necessary. She learned to mix and blend colours, to shade her eyelids so expertly that even the agency's own beautician couldn't do better. She learned to avoid extremes of temperatures on her face, to use creams to care for her skin, and to exercise regularly to keep herself supple for the long and often arduous demands of her profession.

During that first year, she had seen little of Max, and when she did see him it was always in the company of someone else. She had quickly realised how insignificant her role was in the agency, and her earlier doubts about Max's motives seemed ridiculous, and vaguely conceited.

By the time she was eighteen, however, the situation had changed. A lucky appearance in a chocolate bar commercial, which had had enormous consumer appeal, catapulted her into the public eye and, like it or not, Max was forced to give her more attention. Suddenly, she was flying off to the Bahamas and Hawaii, taking part in fashion shows and making public appearances, and the consequent raise in salary enabled her to buy her own place.

She had made it, she thought delightedly, walking round her own two-bedroomed apartment, with its windowed living-room overlooking the whole of London, and its step-in bath, with built-in jacuzzi. She had really made it. And all on her own merits. Or so she had thought...

And that was when Max had made his move. Looking back on it now, Abby wondered how she could have been naïve enough not to see what was happening. Of course, he couldn't have approached her when she was younger. For one thing, he would have been risking more than his reputation, and besides, she would most definitely have refused him. What would she have had to lose, after all? What you had never had, you never missed, and her own integrity was still intact.

But by the time she was eighteen she had had a taste of what success could be like. She had dipped her toes into sun-warmed waters, and basked in the glow of public acclaim. She had grown used to choosing her clothes without always thinking about the price, and parked outside her new apartment was the sleek red Porsche she had paid the deposit on with half of her last cheque.

All these thoughts ran wildly through her head the afternoon Max invited her to spend the weekend on his yacht. It wasn't a party, he said smoothly, leaving her in no doubt as to his intentions. Just an opportunity for them to get to know one another better. And Abby, who had heard the gossip from time to time about the girls who had been invited to spend some time on the *Xerxes*, knew there was no mistake.

But, naturally, she demurred. She had other plans, she said. Break them, he replied. But she was very fond of the young man in question, she added. Fonder of him than of her career? Max countered, and Abby faced the unpalatable truth.

She guessed he knew all about her friendship with Andrew Garvey, knew that so far their relationship was as innocent as she was. Abby didn't sleep around. Her associations with men had all been light and fleeting, and Andrew was the first real boyfriend she had had. Was that another reason Max had chosen this moment to pounce? Because he was afraid that if she and Andrew became lovers she might be prepared to give up her career?

If he had only known, Abby thought now. But, nevertheless, she had fought to retain her innocence.

'I don't want to spend the weekend with you, Mr Cervantes,' she declared, with a carefully contrived coolness. 'Thank you for the offer, but no, thanks.'

She remembered Max's lips had curled at this point. He must have known her better than she knew herself. No matter how she might cringe now from the memory of her naïveté, nothing could alter the fact that she had mortgaged her soul.

'I don't think you understand,' Max said then, inviting her to sit down in the comfortable visitor's chair that faced his own across the mahogany expanse of his desk. And when she was seated, albeit unwillingly, 'This invitation is non-returnable. Must I remind you of your contract with the agency? You agreed to accept any assignment I, as your employer, should decide was suitable.'

Abby's chest heaved. 'This is *not* an assignment!'

'And if I choose to say it is?'

'I won't do it.'

Max shrugged. 'That is your prerogative, of course. But I must inform you that if you don't, I shall sever all contracts forthwith, and you will never work for this agency again.'

Abby's breath came out in a painful gasp. 'You wouldn't.'

Max regarded her stoically. 'Wouldn't I?'

Abby licked her lips. 'I—I'll get a job with another agency, then.'

'Which one? When I tell them how you refused to accept a perfectly reasonable assign——'

'It's not perfectly reasonable. It's—it's outrageous!'

'It's life,' replied Max laconically. 'And believe me, Abby, you could be asked a lot worse. At least I like my sex straight. You won't be asked to indulge in any perversity as my mistress.'

'Your mistress!' Abby stared at him. 'You're not serious!'

'Try me.' Max's lips twisted. 'I suggest you give it some consideration. Unless you fancy going back to being a hotel receptionist, of course.'

Abby was sure she could outwit him. During the next few days, she toured the agencies, sounding out her chances of working for a rival concern. But Max had been busy, too, and by Friday afternoon she had had no luck, with the weekend looming ahead of her, grim and unforgiving.

Of course, she could have refused to have anything to do with him, Abby reflected now. She could have told him what he could do with his 'assignment' and walked out of the agency. But she didn't. Oh, it was easy to moralise after the event. It was easy to say that she should have stuck to her guns, and abandoned her only chance of success. Some might say that she could have found success in another field, but Abby had been brought up in a harder school, where you didn't slap a gift horse in the mouth. The chances of her finding another career with so many opportunities was as unlikely as Max's showing her some sympathy. And because she was young—and ambitious—she steeled her nerve and took her medicine.

It didn't work. In spite of Max's best efforts to get her to respond to his lovemaking, he was eventually forced to abandon the attempt. She was cold—*frigid*, he informed her scathingly. She didn't have a sexual emotion in her body. All she was was a beautiful shell, promising all, but giving nothing.

For a while, after that awful weekend was over, Abby worried about what would happen now, but her fears proved groundless. Even though their personal relationship had failed, Max was too much of a businessman to dispose of his best asset. On the contrary, with his support, her career went from strength to strength, and by the time she was twenty Max could no longer claim she needed his backing to survive. She was a success in her own right; she was offered work all over the world. And when she went to New York for that year's spring collections she was probably the most famous face on the fashion scene.

Not that she had had any intention of leaving Max, at that time. In actual fact, their association had never been better. Now that the spectre of his sexual interest in her had been removed, their relationship had resumed its earlier promise, and, if anyone had asked her, Abby would probably have said that Max was her friend. They often dined together these days, sharing their common interest in the agency's success, and discussing possible plans for the future. Abby had learned a lot during the past four years, and Max valued her opinion.

Then, on that fateful trip to New York, at a party in Manhattan, Abby had met Jake Lowell.

It wasn't one of the formal gatherings, organised by the fashion industry. Indeed, Abby wouldn't have been there at all if it hadn't been for Max. But he had been invited because their host was an old schoolfriend, and

he had asked Abby to join him because he needed a
female companion.

The party was held in a rather exclusive duplex on
Fifth Avenue. Max's old schoolfriend just happened to
be a New York banker, and most of his guests were
winners, in one field or another. There was a lot of talk
about multi-million-dollar deals, and designer names
were being thrown about, like so much confetti. The fact
that some of the guests were the faces behind those designer names did not impress Abby. In actual fact, she
was bored and, had Max not been enjoying himself, she
would have asked if they could leave.

And then, as she was sipping her second glass of
champagne, and trying rather wearily to show some
interest in the young account executive who had been
trying to chat her up for the last fifteen minutes, she
lifted her eyes and saw Jake. He had evidently just arrived, for he was standing in the doorway, speaking to
their hostess, a rather angular-looking woman wearing
a silver-sequined sheath. She was clinging to his arm,
and it was obvious from her expression that she was
trying, albeit unsuccessfully, to sustain his attention. But
when Jake saw Abby his interest shifted, and, excusing
himself from the too eager hands that detained him, he
made his way across the room towards her. On the way
he gathered a glass of champagne, which he swallowed
so quickly that he couldn't possibly have tasted it, and
Abby's heartbeat quickened as he narrowed the space
between them.

It was strange, but every fibre of her being was
prickling with awareness, and Abby didn't know why.
Oh, he was good to look at, she supposed, although until
then she had never really regarded men in that light. Her
experience with Max had left her cold and distinctly
cynical, and she had never been given any reason to
doubt that his assessment of her sexuality—or lack of
it—was true. Until now.

And then, just when she was steeling herself to face whatever approach he intended to make, his eyes switched to the young man at her side. 'Tom,' he said, shaking the hand Abby's companion eagerly extended. 'It's good to see you.'

'And you, Jake.' The young man flushed, and Abby guessed this must be someone of importance. Another high-roller, she estimated ruefully. How could she ever have imagined she'd be interested in him? Oh, there was no denying he was attractive, in a tough, hard-boned kind of way, and she had no doubt that most women would jump at the chance of getting to know him better. But, as it was equally obvious from the way he was scanning the rest of the room that he wasn't interested in her either, she mentally shrugged away any lingering traces of regret on both scores.

However, her companion was much less perceptive. 'I guess you don't know Abby, do you, Jake?' he asked, causing Abby to give an inward groan at his naïveté. 'Abby—Stuart,' Tom added, quite unnecessarily. 'Jake Lowell.'

'How do you do?' Abby offered the usual acknowledgement, hoping Jake didn't imagine she had engineered this introduction. But she didn't offer to shake hands. She had been the recipient of too many sweaty palms to fall into that particular trap, even though she doubted Jake Lowell's temperature had risen by so much as a degree.

'Hi.'

His response was even shorter than her own, though his eyes lingered now, and Abby felt a wave of perspiration envelop her. Although the apartment was warm, it was an inner heat that attacked her sensory glands and made even the off-the-shoulder bodice of her dress cling with sudden energy to her skin.

'Abby's a model,' Tom inserted enthusiastically, apparently unaware of any tension in the air. 'She works for that guy, Max Cervantes. Do you know Cervantes, Jake?'

'We've met,' essayed Jake Lowell evenly, without taking his eyes from Abby. 'But, as I understand it, Miss Stuart doesn't work *for* Cervantes. He works for her.'

Abby's lips parted. 'I don't think Max would like to hear you say that,' she murmured ruefully, feeling an unexpected surge of relief to know he had a sense of humour. She almost wanted to laugh out loud at his outrageous comment, even though she knew it had not been that funny. Nevertheless, a burst of adrenalin was running through her veins, and it was all she could do to restrain her excitement.

'No,' Jake admitted now, sharing her amusement. 'I don't suppose he would. But then, I won't tell him, if you don't.'

'Well, anyway, Abby works for the Cervantes agency,' put in Tom, somewhat resentfully. He didn't like the way the other two seemed to be enjoying a joke at his expense, and in his irritation he put a possessive hand on Abby's shoulder.

It was a mistake. Abby usually avoided being touched by anyone, and most of all by casual acquaintances at parties. With a delibrate shrug of her shoulder, she dislodged his hand, but as she endeavoured to put some distance between them she inadvertently came up against the strength of Jake's hard frame.

The effect was electric. Whereas when Tom had touched her she had felt an instinctive revulsion to the contact, Jake's firm body inspired no such reaction. On the contrary, when his arm came automatically to support her momentary imbalance she knew a quite unfamiliar desire to lean against him.

'Oh—I'm sorry,' she murmured, stepping away from him, even though the urge to stay where she was was almost overwhelming, and Jake smiled down at her. It was quite a novelty for Abby not to be on eye-level terms with a man, and she smiled in return, her breath quickening in concert with her pulses.

'No problem.' Jake's curiously golden eyes dispelled her embarrassment. His lips twisted. 'As a matter of fact, I enjoyed it.'

Tom's face was quite red now, and Abby guessed that only his awareness of Jake Lowell's influence—whatever it might be—was keeping him from making some aggressive comment. But then, before anything untoward could happen, a fourth person joined their circle, his sharp blue eyes instantly assessing what was going on here.

'Abby,' he said, and this time there was no escaping the possessiveness of the hand that gripped her upper arm. 'I've been looking for you.'

'Have you?'

Abby turned to Max with scarcely concealed impatience. He knew how she resented his proprietorial attitude towards her, though perhaps in the circumstances he thought he was doing her a favour.

'Yes.' Max's gaze moved over the two men who were present, and his lips twitched. 'Lowell,' he acknowledged coolly. 'Anderson.' Then, to Abby, 'Are you enjoying yourself?'

'Very much.' Abby nodded, her own eyes meeting Jake's for a moment before sliding away. 'Are you?'

'I am now.' Max had to tilt his head slightly to look up at her, and his eyes narrowed. 'But you already know that, don't you?'

Abby's face flamed, but before she could frame a reply Max spoke again. 'Actually, there's someone I want you to meet. Sloane Maxwell. Come along. I'll introduce you.'

'Right now?'

Abby stood her ground, trying to act as if her behaviour was in no way out of character, and Max's mouth tightened. 'Yes, right now,' he insisted, his voice losing its indulgence. 'Gentlemen.' He nodded to her two companions. 'You will excuse us, won't you?'

Jake, who hadn't said a thing, not even when Max had offered his indifferent greeting, suddenly intervened. 'Perhaps the lady is enjoying herself right here,' he remarked, spreading his feet, and folding his arms across the not inconsiderable width of his chest. Beside Max's short, rotund figure, he looked fit and powerful, his attitude in every way superior to that of the older man. 'Why don't you ask her?' he suggested. 'Let Abby choose.'

Max's face went red now. 'Why don't you butt out, Lowell?' he retorted angrily, and even Tom Anderson backed away from the unexpected antagonism in his voice. 'This is not your concern.'

'Perhaps I'm making it my concern,' replied Jake smoothly, apparently unperturbed by Max's rudeness. 'The lady has an opinion. Why don't you let her air it?'

'Why don't you mind your own business?' countered Max furiously. 'Miss Stuart is my guest. Get out of my way, or I'll—I'll——'

'You'll what?' Jake's lips curled. 'Come on. D'you want to make something of this?'

'No!' Abby's intervention was heartfelt. But the last thing she wanted was to instigate a fight between these two men. Not that she imagined it would be much of a contest—physically, at least. But Max was not opposed to fighting dirty, as she well knew, and, however stupid it seemed, she did not want Jake Lowell to learn of their relationship like this. 'Please,' she added, putting a reluctant hand through Max's arm. 'It's quite all right, Mr Lowell——'

'Jake.'

'Jake, then, but I really do have to go. It—it was very nice to meet you. Perhaps—some other time...'

She hoped the appealing look she cast in his direction as Max guided her away reassured him that she didn't blame him for what had happened. She wished with all her heart that Max had not interrupted them, but common sense told her that this was not the place to make a stand. For some reason Max disliked the handsome American and, although it was disappointing, she had really had no choice.

CHAPTER SIX

HOWEVER, it was not so easy to forget that moment when Jake had put his arm around her. For the first time in her life, Abby had actually welcomed a man's touch, and the remembrance of the electricity that had sprung between them kept her awake for hours after Max had gone to his room.

Of course, it hadn't been easy convincing Max that she had not been attracted to the other man. He was still brooding over the way Jake had acted, and it had taken a concerted effort on Abby's part not to look in Jake's direction for the rest of the evening. Not that she was *afraid* of Max, she told herself firmly, as she shed her clothes prior to going to bed. But he could be spiteful on occasion, and it was just unfortunate that the only man she had ever noticed should be someone Max didn't like.

The phone rang as she was rearranging her pillows for the umpteenth time. For once, the splendid luxury of the suite the agency had provided for her at the Helmsley Palace had lost its appeal, and, although she was tired, she couldn't relax.

And then the phone rang, and all her nerves rang with it. Who could it be? she wondered. It was almost four o'clock in the morning. The only person she could think of was Max, and the possibilities of that eventuality didn't bear thinking about.

She wondered if she should ignore it, pretend she hadn't heard it, bury her head in the pillow and feign sleep, but her curiosity got the better of her. Leaning out of bed, she picked up the gold-rimmed receiver, and, putting it to her ear, she said huskily, 'Yes?'

'Abby?'

The voice should not have been familiar, but it was. Swallowing convulsively, she struggled up against the pillows and took a breath. 'Mr. Lowell,' she whispered. 'Do you know what time it is?'

'Is that the only reason you're whispering?' he enquired drily, and she caught her breath.

'I beg your pardon.'

'I mean—are you alone?' he appended flatly, and, although she knew an initial sense of indignation, it was not such an outrageous question in the circumstances.

'I—of course I'm alone,' she answered swiftly. 'It's four o'clock in the morning. What—what do you want?'

'I don't think I ought to answer that, on the grounds that it might incriminate me,' he replied, his voice deepening attractively. 'How about if I ask you to have breakfast with me? Then we can talk about what we want of one another.'

Abby's breath escaped on a gasp. 'Breakfast?' she echoed. 'But it's the middle of the night!'

'But you're not sleeping, and nor am I,' Jake returned easily. 'OK, I'll give you a couple of hours to get ready. I'll meet you in the lobby of your hotel at 6 a.m. How about that?'

'6 a.m.!' Abby shook her head bewilderedly. 'But there's nowhere open at 6 a.m.'

'Don't you believe it,' Jake told her softly. 'See you!' And with that, he rang off.

She knew she should have cleared it with Max first. She knew it was madness to leave her hotel in the early hours of the morning, to meet a man she knew absolutely nothing about. Oh, it was obvious that, as he had attended the party the night before, he was someone of some consequence, but she supposed the most unscrupulous villains in New York could masquerade behind a mask of respectability. Besides which, Max had evidently disliked the man, and she should have trusted his judgement before her own.

But she didn't. Acting purely on instinct, she followed the dictates of her own heart, convincing herself she had nothing to lose that she hadn't already lost.

He was waiting for her when she emerged from the lift. Not knowing where he was taking her, she had opted for black tights, and a thigh-length cashmere sweater, whose creamy colour matched the highlights in her hair. And she was glad she had dressed informally when she saw his jeans and leather jacket. Like her, he had anticipated the chill of an early April morning, and as he came to meet her she was again struck by his unconscious attraction.

'Hi,' he said, the look he gave her causing an unexpected shiver to tingle up her spine. 'Did you miss me?'

'Miss you?' Abby was confused, and Jake grinned.

'I missed you,' he conceded, tucking his hand beneath her elbow. 'But then, I've had more time to do so. I haven't been to bed.'

He didn't look as if he hadn't been to bed. Indeed, his golden eyes, hooded by thick black lashes, looked every bit as alert as they had done the night before, his lean face showing no hint of weariness in its dark-skinned contours. She suspected he was a man who had a hard core of inner strength—or was it ruthlessness? She couldn't be sure.

'Where—where are we having breakfast?' she asked, as they crossed the lobby under the watchful eye of the night concierge, and Jake's hand at her elbow tightened.

'Central Park,' he said equably, prepared for her instinctive reaction, and not being disappointed.

'Central Park?' she echoed, trying without any success to pull away from him. 'But—isn't that dangerous?'

'I don't think so,' replied Jake, nodding to the doorman, who opened the door for them, and Abby realised there was no turning back when the reinforced glass thudded heavily behind them.

They had the best hot Danishes Abby had ever tasted at a coffee stand at the edge of the park. And, although initially she had been a little apprehensive, the awareness of the two burly individuals who tailed them reassured her that Jake was not completely reckless. It was her first introduction to protective surveillance, though she soon learned that Jake had a constant bodyguard all the time he was in New York.

By the time he delivered her back to her hotel, Max was awake and asking for her. And he was furious when he learned where she had been. 'You must be mad,' he exclaimed coldly, 'going out with a man you know nothing about! This is New York, Abby, not Egham! Anything could have happened to you.'

'Like what?' Abby was still high after the intoxicating hours she had spent with Jake, and in no mood to be discouraged. 'What could he do to me that you've not already done?' she demanded, with some bitterness. 'He likes me, and I like him. And don't try to stop me seeing him again, or—or——'

'Or what, Abby?' Max's lips were tight.

'There are—other agencies, you know,' she replied at last, realising exactly what she was risking for the sake of a man she still hardly knew. 'Don't make me do it, Max. We both know we need one another.'

In the days that followed, Abby saw Jake many times. Although she was left in no doubt as to Max's disapproval, he made no further attempt to stop her meeting the other man, and whenever she was free Jake either came himself, or sent his chauffeur, to pick her up from the hotel.

He took her dining, and dancing; he even took her to the ballet once, at her suggestion, though he himself had no interest in the art form. Whatever she asked for, he gave her, and by the time she was due to go back to England their relationship had developed to a point of no return.

Not that Jake had touched her. On the contrary, apart from the rather chaste kisses he gave her on leaving her at the hotel, there had been little physical contact between them. It was as if he had sensed her aversion to being touched, although with him she had not felt that instinctive drawing back. Nevertheless, she had been grateful for his sensitivity, and, if she sometimes wondered what it would be like to be touched and caressed by a man she both liked and admired, she was not sufficiently convinced of its desirability to precipitate that kind of crisis.

However, the night before the flight back to London, Abby couldn't sleep. That evening, Jake had taken her to see a currently successful Broadway musical, and afterwards they had had supper at an Italian restaurant. It had been a wonderful evening, and she had been sure Jake would ask her to go back to his apartment. But he hadn't. Instead, he had delivered her back to her hotel as usual, with the only proviso being that he would join her at the airport in the morning, prior to the Concorde flight to London.

So he was going to see her off, Abby thought unhappily. Another cool kiss, probably in Max's presence, and a casual farewell before she boarded the plane. Not exactly what she had had in mind, she admitted, even if the idea of going to bed with *any* man was still anathema to her. But she had hoped he would have wanted to. Or was she so unattractive she turned him off?

But that couldn't be true, she argued, pacing about her hotel suite. You didn't wine and dine someone on at least a dozen different occasions unless you enjoyed their company. Or did you? She was so confused. So bewildered that it should end like this.

The idea of ringing him and asking him to join her for breakfast came out of the blue. He had given her a number she could call, and while, as she had never used it, she didn't know if it was the number of his office or his apartment, the notion of using it rapidly took growth. But not yet, she decided, glancing at her watch and discovering it was barely two o'clock. She would wait at least another four hours, if only to convince him she hadn't spent a sleepless night.

By the time she did pick up the phone, however, second, and even third thoughts were threatening to defeat her. She had to dial the number very quickly before apprehension, and lack of confidence, forced her to put it down again, and when a *woman* answered she very nearly cut the call.

'I—wanted to speak to—Mr Lowell,' she eventually admitted, telling herself it could be his mother, or his sister, or his secretary she was speaking to, and the woman sighed.

'It is only six-thirty, Miss—Ms—er...?'

'I know,' said Abby, not giving her name as the woman expected. 'Um—who am I speaking to, please?'

'This is Mr Lowell's answering service,' replied the woman shortly, clearly not pleased that Abby had turned the tables. 'Who shall I tell Mr Lowell is calling? I'm afraid if you don't give me your name, I can't deliver the message.'

'Oh...' Abby was so relieved that it was not some woman living in Jake's apartment that for a moment she could hardly speak. 'I—er—my name's Stuart. *Miss* Stuart.'

'Got it.' The woman sounded resigned now. 'I'll give Mr Lowell the message, and have him call you back. He does know the number, I guess. Am I right?'

'Well—yes.' Abby licked her lips. 'But—can't I speak to him?'

'This is just an answering service, Miss Stuart.' The woman evidently thought she was stupid, by her tone. 'As I say, I'll give Mr Lowell the message. If he doesn't get back to you, hey! It's not my fault.'

When Abby replaced the receiver on its stand, she was convinced she had made the biggest mistake of her life. It was one thing to ring Jake and ask him if he'd like to have breakfast with her, and quite another to speak to some anonymous answering service, who might pass on her message halfway through the morning. And what would Jake think, hearing she had been trying to get in touch with him? Oh, it was so embarrassing! She had a good mind to call the answering service again, and cancel the call.

Her hand was actually reaching for the receiver when the phone rang. For a moment she couldn't believe it, and just sat there staring at the machine, as if she were imagining the whole thing. But then the realisation that the bell had rung at least half a dozen times already sent her stretching for the handset, removing it from its cradle and lifting it to her ear. 'Yes?'

'Abby?' It was Jake, and she sank down weakly on to the side of the bed before her legs gave out on her completely. 'Abby, is that you?'

'Yes.' Her mouth was dry, but she managed to articulate the word. 'Yes. Yes, it's me. I—I hope you don't mind my using that number you gave me. I didn't realise it was an answering service, or I wouldn't have——'

'What did you want, Abby?' Jake's voice was both mildly impatient, and incredibly gentle. 'Is something wrong? Is that bastard Cervantes threatening you or something? Abby, you don't have to worry about pleasing him any more. You don't need him, and he knows it. You're an independent woman.'

Abby swallowed. 'It—that is—my ringing you has nothing to do with Max.' She frowned, as if just realising the significance of what he had said. 'Why did you mention him?'

'Never mind that.' Jake was unmistakably impatient now. 'Abby, tell me why you rang. You're driving me crazy!'

Abby's lips parted. 'Am I?' For a moment, the idea that she could drive Jake crazy was totally diverting. But then, aware of his impatience, she put the thought aside for more serious consideration later, and added softly, 'I wanted to ask you if you'd like to have breakfast with me.'

Thirty minutes later, she was on her way to Jake's apartment. She had barely had time to take a shower and dress in the suit of heathery Donegal tweed she had been planning to wear on the plane home, before Jake's chauffeur appeared at the hotel.

Her original plan, that Jake should come to the hotel and have breakfast with her there, had been revised. Better that she should come to his apartment, Jake had said smoothly. At least there, Max would not be able to interrupt them, and Abby had been unable to think of a single convincing objection.

All the same, she was a little apprehensive. It was she who had made the call, after all, and she hoped Jake did not imagine she was in the habit of doing such a thing.

It was her first visit to his apartment, although she had seen the enormous skyscraper many times as she had driven along Park Avenue. Even so, it was daunting to enter a lift that didn't stop until the fiftieth floor. Daunting, too, to know that she had no control over its operation, that, unless Jake pressed the necessary buttons, the lift would not return her to the street.

The doors of the lift opened on to a marble-floored hallway, with a huge chandelier, and a carved oak staircase curving to an upper storey. Although she knew this was the penthouse apartment, she had not expected

it to be so quiet up here, but the apartment had a sepul-
chral hush at this hour of the morning.

And then a door opposite opened, and a strange man
appeared, and for a moment Abby was afraid she had
made a terrible mistake. But the man smiled, and said
politely, 'Miss Stuart, won't you please follow me?' and
she realised her mistake—if she had made one—had not
been one of location.

Her impressions of the apartment on that occasion
were brief but overwhelming. Thick velvet carpets that
cushioned the feet, and were no doubt partly responsible
for the distinct hush, cradled a fortune in wood and
leather. She saw rooms that were as big as her whole
apartment back in London, and, although Abby was no
expert, she knew the paintings alone would have bought
a whole string of penthouses such as this, should Jake
have chosen to sell them. She saw long windows, cur-
tained in pure silk, that gave a view of the whole skyline
of Manhattan, and she wondered how anyone living in
such surroundings could fail to feel superior to the rest
of humanity. It was a rich man's home, a millionaire's
retreat, and proof—if proof were needed—that Jake was
no ordinary mortal.

But for the present she followed the manservant up
the carved staircase, her heels echoing noisily on the
gleaming treads. Panelled walls mounted with her to a
galleried landing, with a skylight that arched above their
heads like the dome of a cathedral. She stepped on to a
soft grey carpet, that flowed into the recesses of half a
dozen double doors, and hesitated nervously when the
manservant approached a particular set of doors and
rapped discreetly.

Abby heard a voice call 'Come!' and then the man-
servant stepped forward, opening the doors with a
flourish, and announcing politely, 'Miss Stuart, sir.'

Of course, Abby had no choice but to go forward then,
though her knees were a little unsteady as she left the

grey carpet for one of burnt ochre. And as the panelled doors closed behind her, with only a shivering draught of air, she found herself in what she quickly realised was Jake's bedroom.

Her initial reaction was one of panic. When she had made that call this morning, she had expected nothing like this, and her own ideas of taking breakfast with him in the dining-room of her hotel, or—more daringly—in the sitting-room of her suite, paled into insignificance beside this piece of recklessness. She had never dreamt she was being conducted to his own private apartments, and her face flushed at the realisation of what the man-servant must have thought of her.

'So what did you expect at seven o'clock in the morning?' Jake enquired lazily, and Abby's gaze travelled across a vast expanse of carpet to where he was lounging on the side of an enormous Colonial-style four-poster. In a dark blue silk dressing-gown, and little else, as far as Abby could see, judging by the bare leg that emerged from the hem of the gown and hung negligently over the side of the bed, he looked more attractive than ever, and infinitely more dangerous. His other leg was drawn up, so that his elbow could rest upon it, and the cloth separated between his legs, giving a glimpse of a dark, hair-roughened thigh.

Dragging her eyes away from that particular danger, Abby took a steadying breath. 'You were dressed long before this the morning you came to my hotel,' she replied, clutching her flat bag like a shield across the upper part of her thighs, and Jake's lips twisted.

'So I was,' he conceded, and then, as she continued to look anywhere but at him, he slid off the bed and came towards her.

His approach, on bare feet, was so silent that for a moment Abby was unaware that he had left the bed. But when his tall, lean figure blocked her view, she started nervously.

'Would you rather I ask Raoul to carry this lot downstairs?' Jake asked gently, gesturing towards the long windows, and now Abby's eyes focused on the table for two which had been laid in the embrasure. Hot coffee steamed above a tiny burner, while an assortment of hot dishes and sweet pastries invited her investigation. There were muffins and hot rolls, fruit of all kinds, and delicately curled swirls of butter in a scalloped dish.

'Oh!' Abby's lips framed a perfect 'o' as she surveyed the exquisitely prepared meal, and, realising she couldn't possibly expect anyone to rearrange it all somewhere else, she shook her head. 'I—no. No, of course not.'

'Good.' Jake caught and held her eyes now, and she felt the overpowering strength of his attraction weakening her objections. 'So—shall we?'

Abby moistened her dry lips with her tongue. 'Why—why not?' she agreed jerkily, and then caught her breath when his hands went to her shoulders, sliding beneath the lapels of her jacket and slipping it off her shoulders.

'I don't think you need this, do you?' he enquired, tossing the jacket over a nearby chair, and, although it had been an innocent enough gesture, Abby's chest rose and fell beneath the rose-coloured silk shirt she had worn with the suit. It made her feel intensely vulnerable suddenly, as if he could see through the silk to the lacy bra beneath, and it took the utmost effort to remain motionless when what she really wanted to do was snatch up the jacket again.

'Hey,' he said suddenly, brushing his knuckle along the curve of her jawline, 'lighten up. You initiated this meeting, you know. So why don't you tell me what's troubling you?'

Abby swallowed. 'N—nothing's troubling me.'

'But you wanted to see me, right?'

Abby took a deep breath. 'Right.'

'Why?' Jake's eyebrow quirked. 'I said I'd see you at the airport, didn't I?'

'Yes, but...'

'But what?'

Abby sighed. 'I just thought—well, that is—Max will be at the airport,' she finished awkwardly, and Jake smiled.

'I see.'

The look Jake was giving her now made her want to cringe. Oh, God! she thought sickly. Now he knows I'm running after him! I should never have rung! I should never have come!

Wanting only to leave now, Abby turned abruptly aside, but before she could reach for her jacket, Jake's hand at her nape prevented her. 'Why didn't you tell me last night?' he asked, his voice low and sensual, and Abby shivered.

'Tell you?' she echoed unsteadily. 'Tell you what?'

'That you want me as much as I want you?' Jake replied huskily. 'God, don't you have any idea of the self-control it's taken to keep my hands off you?'

Abby turned her head, feeling no revulsion at the hard strength of his fingers on her neck. 'But—I thought——'

'Yes? What did you think?' Jake's free hand came to stroke the satiny curve of her cheek.

'But I'm leaving for London in—in three hours.'

'So am I,' said Jake simply, and she stared at him.

'You are?'

'Of course. You didn't think I intended it to end as of last night, did you?'

Abby couldn't take it in. 'You didn't?' she whispered foolishly, and his eyes darkened to a vibrant amber.

'No,' he declared flatly. 'I'm not that altruistic. I want you, Abby. I've never wanted any woman as I want you. But there's something about you.' His thumbs caressed her cheekbones. 'I don't know what it is, exactly, but you seem—untouched, somehow. Or should I say *untouchable*?' He didn't notice the faint colour that invaded her cheeks at his words, or, if he did, he put it down to what he was saying. 'I've not wanted to rush you, to *scare* you. There was no way I was going to blow a relationship that I think could become something big, something important, for both of us.'

Abby quivered, and his hands slid to cup her neck, invading the neckline of her shirt, and discovering the fragile strap of her bra. His hands were immensely strong, but immensely gentle, stroking the sensitive flesh and turning her limbs to water.

'Tell me,' he went on softly, 'how is it that someone who looks so amazingly confident on the catwalk can make me feel as if I'm touching a virgin? You're not a virgin, are you, Abby? I couldn't be that lucky.'

Abby hesitated, and then shook her head. 'No.'

'No.' Jake repeated her denial half regretfully, and then nodded. 'But it was a long time ago, right?'

Abby gulped. 'Yes.'

'And he—hurt you, didn't he?' Jake continued huskily, bending his head to brush his lips across her ear.

Abby's breath came out on a quavering sigh. 'Yes.'

'I knew it.' Jake sounded almost triumphant now. 'I knew there was something—something about you that was different. God,' his mouth compressed angrily now, 'how could anybody hurt you? It's just as well he's not around any more. I could kill him!'

Abby moved her head helplessly from side to side. 'Don't—don't say that.'

'Why not?' Jake looked at her intently. 'Did you love him? Do you *still* love him?'

'Oh, no.' Abby was very definite about that. 'No, I—I never loved him. It's just that——'

'—that you don't like hurting anybody, right?' Jake finished for her gently. 'OK, OK. We'll forget about him. It's we who matter. You and I that are important.' His fingers traced the unknowing sensitive contours of her

ear as he lowered his lips to touch her cheek. 'I'll just
have to be much more patient, hmm? But don't be afraid
of me. I'd never hurt you.'

Abby trembled, the brush of his tongue against her
skin a potent stimulation. But, deep inside her, she was
very much afraid she was going to disappoint him.
Remembering the way she had felt when Max had
touched her, she couldn't suppress a sudden sense of
withdrawal, but when she would have drawn away Jake's
hands on her shoulders prevented her.

'Relax,' he said easily, sensing her confusion, and she
looked up at him helplessly, torn by her conflicting emotions. She wanted to make love with Jake; she wanted
to give herself to him, and know that they were together;
but she didn't believe it was possible. Sooner or later,
he would want to do to her what Max had done, and,
while she did not feel any revulsion at his kisses and
caresses, she was already panicking at the thought of
anything else. It had been so long since her experiences
with Max, and she knew that over the years her body
had steeled itself against a physical invasion. She was
like a tool that had been used and abused and left to go
rusty, and, because the man who used it first had dis-
torted the mechanism, no amount of patience could
really put it right.

'You don't understand,' she said now, putting up her
hands to grip his wrists, unaware of how tightly she was
gripping him, or that her nails were digging into his flesh.
'I don't think I can—that is—I want to, but—well, I
think I'm—frigid.'

If she had expected some horrified ejaculation from
Jake, she was disappointed. On the contrary, instead of
looking anxious, he half smiled. 'Really?' he said, easing
her nails away from his skin, and causing her to release
him with some embarrassment. 'Abby, I don't believe
that. You're far too responsive. You just had a bad
experience, that's all. Do you want me to convince you?'

Abby licked her lips again, and this time while she did so Jake leant towards her, and touched her tongue with his own. It was a startling experience, and Abby's tongue disappeared into her mouth again with rapid haste. But she could still taste the slightly peppermint-flavoured cleanness of his mouth, and unknowingly she savoured it when he abruptly turned away from her.

'Food,' he said, gesturing towards the table, but Abby knew that the idea of trying to eat anything was beyond her. Instead, she wished she had the confidence to go after him, and put her arms around him, the simple pleasure of pressing her face against his back a desperate aspiration.

When she neither moved, nor said anything, Jake turned back to her, and now she saw the sudden strain that marked his face. It was as if he, too, was desperate for something he couldn't have, and she gazed at him despairingly, wishing she could help.

'Don't, for pity's sake, look at me like that!' he said, his voice suddenly harsh, and Abby blinked her bewilderment. 'For heaven's sake,' he added, 'you can't be that naïve! Go—have some breakfast. I need a shower. A cold one for preference.'

Abby took a step forward. 'Jake——'

'Don't worry,' he said, aware of her confusion and trying to reassure her, 'I won't be long. Have some eggs, or some coffee. Raoul will be disappointed if you don't try his cooking——'

'I don't want anything to eat,' Abby said firmly, taking another step towards him. 'Jake—please; don't go. I'm sorry if I seem a mess, but I don't know what I can do about it.'

'Abby!' His use of her name was grim, but looking at him Abby could see that he wasn't really angry—at least, not with her.

With a determination she had not known she possessed, until now, she covered the space between them, hesitating only a moment before stepping closer and sliding her arms around his neck. 'Kiss me,' she breathed, her heart palpitating so loudly, she was sure that he must hear it. 'Please.'

Jake's jaw hardened, the muscles jerking as he struggled for control, but his body betrayed him. Almost convulsively, his hands moved to the slender curve of her waist, and, because her face was tilted up to his, it was a simple matter to join his lips to hers.

Abby stiffened automatically at the touch of his lips; the way she always did, she realised, even when he kissed her goodnight. Which was probably why their relationship had never progressed beyond this point, she acknowledged unhappily. She just didn't have the ability any more, to give herself to anyone. If she ever had ...

But, when she would have drawn back, Jake wouldn't let her. Instead of letting her go, as he had always done before, his hands left her waist to cup her face, and his tongue probed insistently at the tightly clenched joining of her mouth. Her breath quickened even more, and she had to physically fight the urge to tear his hands away from her face. This wasn't what she wanted, she decided urgently. Nothing was worth the churning panic he was creating.

She had to stop him, and, short of actually fighting with him, she had to speak. But when she parted her lips to do so his tongue forced its way into her mouth, and the kiss which had been so dry and chaste became hot and wet and sensual.

Abby's legs went suddenly weak, and, although her mind was still telling her she had to get away from him, her emotions were telling her something else. As the passionate assault continued, a curious heat flowered in the pit of her stomach, and as Jake continued to hold her it began to spread up over her stomach to her breasts, and down through the muscles of her thighs.

She was trembling now, but it was not with fear, she realised. The heat that was engulfing her body was alerting her to the awareness of Jake's nearness, to the sensual heat of his body where it brushed against her own, and to the clean smell of his arousal that filled her with anticipation.

'Dear God,' he groaned at last, when he released her mouth to seek the scented hollow of her throat, and Abby abandoned all inhibitions and pressed herself against him. She wanted to be close to him; she wanted to feel his strength.

As he sensed her excitement, Jake's fingers came to unbutton her shirt, separating the soft cloth to expose the generous roundness of her breasts. For once, Abby was glad her breasts were not the diminutive molehills so admired by her fellow models. Released from the lacy bra, they filled Jake's hands with their burgeoning fullness, and he buried his face in their swollen beauty.

And with every sensuous action Abby could feel the excitement inside her growing. She didn't want to escape from Jake; Jake's lovemaking didn't fill her with loathing. On the contrary, she was discovering a part of herself she had not known existed, and when his fingers found the zipper on her skirt, and he released it to send the skirt shimmying over her hips, she felt no real shame as she stood there in only her silk panties and stockings.

'You—are beautiful,' said Jake unsteadily, looking down at her, and Abby found the strength to meet his gaze.

'Am I?'

'Most—definitely,' he said, glancing over his shoulder at the bed. 'Come on. Let me finish undressing you. I think we'll make it easier over here.'

He sat her down on the side of the bed, and then, with the utmost sensitivity, he knelt in front of her and drew her panties down over her hips. Urging her to lie back for a moment, on her elbows, he eased the lacy scrap of silk under her hips, and then pulled it off completely and tossed it aside. The stockings followed, and, although Abby was a little less confident now, the surging heat of her body which seemed to have centred itself in a moist core between her legs gave her the ability to sit still under his hands.

'Beautiful,' he said again when she was completely naked, stroking a sensuous finger from the swollen tip of her breast, down over her quivering diaphragm and flat stomach to the curly cleft that throbbed beneath his touch. 'God, Abby,' he added, loosening the cord of his dressing-gown and allowing it to part and expose his own nakedness. 'I want you!'

Abby shifted across the bed as he came down beside her, her nerves jerking anxiously now that she was confronted with the inevitable fact of his intentions. He was so big, she acknowledged tremulously, never having seen a man's body so fully aroused before. When Max had touched her, she had closed her eyes. Clenched them tightly shut, she remembered painfully. Hating him, and hating herself for submitting to his demands.

'Take it easy,' Jake whispered now, and she knew that once again he had apprehended her anxiety. With what she later acknowledged was consummate skill, he sought her twitching lips and covered them with his mouth, soothing her apprehensions with the sensual possession of his tongue.

Within seconds, she was responding to him again, her hand moving up to the smooth curve of his shoulder, revelling in the tactile pleasure of touching his muscled flesh. His body was so firm and hard and masculine, not pale and soft as Max's had been, and, regaining her excitement, she let her hand explore further.

Below his shoulders, his body curved in to a narrow waist and hips, the hard bones of his pelvis taut beneath the velvet skin. His legs were long, and lightly covered with fine dark hair, much like the triangle on his chest that arrowed down below his navel. There were curls of dark hair lower on his body, that brushed against her thigh, and the pulsating shaft that throbbed against her leg.

Meanwhile, Jake was exploring her body equally as thoroughly. The first time he took her hard nipple into his mouth and suckled on it she started violently, but by the time he progressed to her other breast she was offering herself to his lips. The sight of his dark head moving against her breast was immensely disturbing. But the feelings he evoked were so delightful, she couldn't believe that it was wrong. All Max had done was squeeze her breasts, painfully. She had never dreamt they could be so sensitive, or that she could get such pleasure from them.

While his mouth was occupied elsewhere, Jake's hands discovered other pursuits, caressing her waist and hips, and the long slender beauty of her legs, and then settling quite naturally between them and urging Abby to move them apart.

'Let me touch you,' he whispered, returning to her mouth with increasing urgency. 'Oh, God, you're really ready for me, sweetheart. Don't make me wait any longer.'

Abby could only move her head helplessly from side to side. Now that the moment had come, she could only think of Max, and she could feel herself stiffening instinctively. But once again Jake was aware of her reactions. Without allowing her to lose the melting sweetness they had been sharing, he parted her legs and gently but insistently pushed himself inside her, stifling her objections with the imperative possession of his mouth.

And Abby's fears were defeated. With his mouth on hers, and the unmistakable fullness of him inside her, her senses tilted. This was not Max, she realised light-headedly, this was Jake. Jake, whom she was almost sure she loved, and who would never hurt her as Max Cervantes had.

And then Jake began to move. Caressing her breasts, and the palpitating curve of her stomach, he almost withdrew from the hot, wet honeycomb that was tight about him, and then plunged in again and repeated the process. And Abby, who had been afraid that she would never respond to any man's lovemaking, felt every nerve in her body tingle. It was as if he was scraping over every sensuous cord in her being, waking her up, bringing her alive, making her want to wind her legs about his body and urge him ever closer.

'Gently,' he muttered hoarsely, and later she was to realise the inordinate amount of will-power it had taken for him to proceed at her pace, and not his own. 'Just— enjoy it,' he added, and she did, so much so that Max, and his machinations, were obliterated completely...

CHAPTER SEVEN

ABBY shivered now at the remembrance of Jake's love-making. It had been so good, so perfect, and for the first time in her life she had experienced the true meaning of making love. There had been no doubts in her mind then. Her fears of frigidity, of being incapable of feeling passion, had been dispelled completely. She had striven for the stars, and reached them, and the mindless aftermath had left her feeling totally at peace.

But not for long. Jake had wanted her too much to be satisfied so easily. Within minutes, he had driven her receptive body to further heights of enchantment, and Abby had lost all sense of self in his eagerly sought possession. She remembered it all so clearly, painfully clearly, she acknowledged now. The spacious room with its huge, comfortable bed; the early morning sky, with the sun streaking grey clouds over the towers of the city; and Jake's urgent body, his hungry kisses, his hot, damp skin, and the potent smell of sex that lingered on the sheets . . .

Of course, perfection didn't last, she admitted bitterly. Although, on that morning, she had thought it would last forever. She remembered how, after their love-making, they had had breakfast in bed. Jake feeding her warm buttered croissants, and the butter trickling down her chin. He had licked it off, she recalled achingly, saying that she was sweeter than any food he had ever tasted. And one thing had led to another, until only Raoul, tapping discreetly on the door, had alerted them to the fact that it was getting late.

They had collected her bags from her hotel, on their way to the airport. Abby had hoped that Max might have left already, but of course he hadn't. When they entered the hotel, they found him pacing angrily about the enormous reception area, and there was no way Abby could avoid a confrontation.

'Where the hell have you been——?' he began, charging towards her, and then he saw Jake behind her, and his approach was arrested.

'Abby's been with me,' Jake replied smoothly, his hand enclosing hers a blatant indication of his possession. 'No problem.'

Max's face contorted, and Abby tensed instinctively. Even though she knew he no longer had any hold over her, that didn't prevent her from feeling apprehensive. She was terrified that Max might say something—or *do* something—in an attempt to destroy her relationship with Jake, and she wished with all her heart that she could have spoken to him first.

Max could be vindictive, as she was well aware, and it was obvious from his expression that he resented the other man's presence. But why? Was he jealous? And why should he have any reason? It wasn't as if their association had ever meant anything to either of them.

Yet, for all that, she had to admit that until now she had never put his feelings to the test. None of the men she had met in the course of her work had ever meant anything to her, and he knew it. Perhaps he had even persuaded himself that there never would be another man for her. After all, he, better than anyone, knew of her aversion to being touched. *He* had inspired that aversion; he had generated it.

Now, ignoring Jake completely, Max turned to Abby. 'Do you realise what time it is?' he demanded, displaying the thick gold watch on his wrist with angry exhortation. 'It's almost a quarter to ten! The flight leaves in less than an hour!'

'We'll make it,' put in Jake calmly, before Abby could make any response. 'I've put my helicopter on stand-by. If you'd like to have the porter load your and Abby's luggage into my car, we can be on our way. Right, Abby?'

'Oh—right.' Abby, who had known nothing about the helicopter, gazed at him bemusedly.

'Thank you, but we would prefer to make our own way to the airport,' Max retorted, ungratefully. 'Abby, the hire car is waiting outside——'

'You'll never make it.' Jake resisted Abby's efforts to release her hand. 'At this hour of the morning, I doubt if you'll even make the bridge before take-off. Accept it, Cervantes: you need my help.'

Max's mouth compressed. 'Then we'll get the later flight,' he declared stubbornly. 'Abby,' he looked at her grimly, 'I want to talk to you.'

'Oh, no.' Once again, Jake intervened. 'Whether you choose to accept my offer is immaterial, except in so far as it means you may have to stay another night in New York. I warn you, it may not be easy to get a seat on tonight's flight. But that's your prerogative. You may please yourself.' He paused. 'But Abby comes with me. Coincidentally, I'm flying to London this morning myself. So—what is your decision? As you say, we don't have a lot of time.'

Max's nostrils flared, and Abby steeled herself for the inevitable outburst, but it never came. Instead, with an unconcealed gesture of frustration, Max snapped his fingers for the porter and ordered him to take his own and Abby's suitcases out to Mr Lowell's limousine.

The journey to the airport was not pleasant. Max had got on board the aircraft first, and manoeuvred himself so that Abby was obliged to sit with him. And, although there was no time for private conversation, he left her in no doubt as to his feelings about her behaviour.

They boarded Concorde with barely five minutes to spare. However, the steward knew Jake, and, although

Abby's seat had been booked beside Max's, she found herself ensconced beside the window with Jake's lean bulk beside her. Max, meanwhile, was obliged to share his journey with a fellow executive, and Abby was happily shielded from the glowering glances he kept casting in their direction.

She and Jake spent the journey finding out about one another. He told her about his sister, and his mother, about his controlling interest in the string of hotels and leisure facilities he had founded, and about the island he owned in the Bahamas, and Sandbar, the house he had built there. His voice changed when he spoke of Sandbar, and she knew that this was somewhere very special to him.

For her part, she gave him an abridged version of her life to date. She told him about being orphaned, and spending the years from six to sixteen in a children's home. She made light of any setbacks she had suffered, not wanting him to feel that she had felt in any way deprived by her circumstances. In fact, she told him all the nice things that had happened, and cheerfully disregarded how tough it had been in the beginning.

When she came to the part about meeting Max, she crossed her fingers and told the first real lie she had ever told. She said that she had been working in a hotel when she saw an advertisement for Max's agency. And, because she now bore little resemblance to the ungainly teenager she had believed herself to be then, Jake believed her when she said that after attending an interview she had been offered the chance to train to become a model.

'And how old were you then?' he asked, as she sipped from her champagne glass, in an effort to disguise her extreme nervousness.

'Sixteen and a half,' she conceded cautiously. 'Why?'

'And you're—how old now? Nineteen? Twenty?' Jake persisted, not answering her question.

'Nearly twenty-one, actually,' she told him. 'Why do you want to know?'

Jake smiled. 'I guess I just wanted to convince myself that Cervantes' possessive attitude towards you is natural,' he admitted, with a grimace. 'I guess if I'd had control of your life for the last four years, I'd feel pretty possessive, too.' He took one of her hands and brought it to his lips, brushing his tongue against her knuckles. 'And I intend to have control of you for a lot longer than that,' he added softly. 'That is if you'll let me.'

The eventual altercation with Max took place the following morning, in his office at the agency. They had arrived in London the previous evening, but Jake's presence had precluded any possibility of a confrontation then. At his suggestion, Abby had accompanied him on the journey into London, and as Max's chauffeur was waiting for him there had been no question of his joining them. Instead, they had driven straight to Abby's apartment, and in the sensual delight of sharing her bed with Jake Abby had forgotten everything but him. However, in the morning light, she was forced to face the fact that sooner or later she was going to have to speak to Max, and tell him how she felt about Jake.

They had spent the night together, and she had awakened that morning to the delicious warmth of Jake's body curled close to hers. His leg had been imprisoning her thighs, as if even in sleep he could not bear to let go of her, and his head had been buried in the hollow of her neck, his breathing warm against her skin. She had never slept with a man before, but it was an experience she was eager to repeat in this case. She had never slept so well, or so soundly, and making love before breakfast was definitely to be recommended.

But she had to put all that to the back of her mind when she entered Max's office later that morning. She had to remember where she was, and who she was with, and not give Max any more ammunition with which to destroy her.

'So,' he said, without getting up from his chair, 'he's made you his mistress.'

The words he used upset her, as she knew they were intended to do. They were a deliberate attempt to denigrate her association with Jake, to put it on the same footing as the demands he had made on her. But she refused to let him see how his cruelty had affected her.

'We are—lovers, yes,' she amended quietly, hoping to avoid any further discussion of what had taken place, but now Max bounded out of his chair, his lips bubbling over with the saliva of his wrath.

'*Lovers!*' he snarled contemptuously, circling the desk towards her like some malevolent spirit. 'What would you know about being a lover? You pathetic little bitch! You may have slept with Mr Hot-shot Lowell, but I bet you're just as sexually stagnant as you ever were!'

'No!'

Abby couldn't prevent the instinctive denial, and Max came closer, his beady eyes glittering dangerously. 'No?'

'No.' Abby stepped back from him, repelled by the cold rapaciousness in his face. 'I—don't wish to talk about it. It's nothing to do with you. It—it's between Jake and me.'

'Like hell it is!' Max's lips curled. 'Come on.' He made a beckoning gesture with his hand. 'Tell me more. After all, I do have a vested interest.'

'No.' Abby pushed the fingers of one hand through the side of her hair. 'Max, please—don't treat me like this. I—I thought we were friends. I—thought you'd be happy for me.'

'No, you didn't.' But Max's initial fury seemed to have abated somewhat. 'You knew how I felt yesterday morning, when that arrogant Yank acted as if *he* owned you, instead of me——'

Abby caught her breath. 'You don't *own* me, Max,' she cried, but he went on as if he hadn't heard her.

'Of course, I don't blame you entirely. Lowell's got what it takes, I can see that. A big car, a fancy apartment; a helicopter, no less! And if you like the Latin type...' He paused reminiscently. 'His family came from South America, did you know that? Probably made their money out of running drugs——'

'That's not true!' Abby couldn't let him go on. 'His father owned a couple of run-down hotels. Jake—Jake borrowed some money and reinvested in modernising the facilities when his father died. He was successful, very successful, and he went on from there. And—and his mother is English.'

'So?' Max spread his hands. 'Did I say she wasn't?'

'No, but——'

'Perhaps you should ask him where he found investors willing to put money into a string of run-down hotels,' declared Max insinuatingly. 'Or perhaps you shouldn't. You're far too valuable to me. I'd hate to see the face— the lovely face—of my top model carved up like a——'

'Stop it!' Abby practically screamed the words at him, but Max, instead of getting mad again, merely pulled a face.

'OK, OK,' he said, evidently well pleased with her reaction. 'We'll say no more about it. Let's forget about Lowell. Who needs him? We've only got a few days before we leave for Bangkok——'

'I—I may not be going.'

Abby's hesitant statement destroyed any chance of a reconciliation. 'What did you say?'

Abby drew a trembling breath. 'I think you heard me.'

'And I hope I didn't.'

Abby licked her lips. 'I said—I may not be going. To Bangkok. Or—or anywhere, for that matter.'

Max's face suffused with colour. 'You're not serious, Abby.'

'I am.' She wrapped the sides of the linen duster about her, and folded her arms about her middle, as if to protect herself from the waves of antagonism emanating from him. 'Jake—Jake wants me to—to be with him.' Her voice broke. 'Surely you can understand that?'

'And you want to be with him, is that it?'

Max's words were spoken so quietly that for a moment Abby wondered if she had imagined them. But there had been no mistake, and, although she was quivering internally, she nodded.

'I see.'

Abby swallowed. 'You mean—you do understand? Oh, Max——'

'It seems as if Lowell had more success than I gave him credit for,' retorted Max, destroying her momentary surge of hope. Instead of going back to his chair he came towards her, capturing her chin with one upraised hand, and turning her face critically towards the light. 'Maybe I gave up too easily,' he added, as she tore herself away from him. 'Did you tell Lowell about us during that heart-to-heart you were having on the plane?'

Abby's response was to charge blindly towards the door, but before her trembling fingers could reach the handle his next words arrested her. 'Perhaps I should have a few words with our American cousin,' he drawled. 'We could compare notes——'

Abby swung round, her shoulders thudding against the panels. 'You—you *wouldn't*!'

'Wouldn't I?'

'But what would you have to gain?' Abby shook her head. 'Do you hate me that much?'

Max's mouth compressed. 'I don't hate you at all, Abby,' he replied, and for once she believed him. 'As a matter of fact, I'm very fond of you, as you well know. And not just because of what we once had——'

Abby caught her breath. 'Max—we had nothing! Nothing!' She lifted her shoulders helplessly. 'I—I was stupid, and you took advantage of me. That's all there was to it.'

'I think the word was—ambitious,' retorted Max coldly. 'You weren't stupid, Abby. You knew exactly what you were doing. You were ambitious. Too ambitious to stop me. And—I guess I did take advantage of that. What man wouldn't?'

Abby took a steadying breath. 'Is that your justification?'

'Do I need one?' Max snorted. 'What does Lowell have to offer in exchange? Marriage?'

Abby bent her head. 'Perhaps.'

The word Max used then was unrepeatable, and, stiffening her shoulders against the door, Abby forced herself to look at him. 'So,' she said, her face unnaturally pale, 'what are you saying? That unless I give Jake up voluntarily, you'll tell him what you did to me? I don't see that that would give you any satisfaction. Might—might I remind you that I—I don't need you any more?'

'Professionally? Perhaps not.' Max shrugged then. 'And, in answer to your question, no. That is not what I am saying.'

'Then what are you saying, damn you?' Abby's voice splintered dangerously. 'For God's sake, Max, what have I ever done to you? Why are you doing this to me?'

'Calm down, calm down.' As if realising he had gone too far, Max moved as if to comfort her, but when she stiffened automatically he circled his desk instead. 'Look,' he said, 'as I see it, we need one another.'

'Do we?'

'As I see it, yes.' Max's expression hardened a little. 'You don't want Lowell to learn of your previous—association with me, and I don't want to lose my best model. I suggest we make a compromise.'

'You mean, I do.' Abby's voice was toneless.

'If you like to see it that way. Very well. I won't be—indiscreet, providing you continue to work for the agency.'

'And—and Jake?'

Max's mouth twitched irritably. 'I can't say I approve of the relationship, but I'll do nothing to stop it—within reason. But marriage—I'm afraid that's out of the question.'

'Why?' Abby's question was almost a sob.

'Marriage brings responsibilities and, God forbid, children! I want none of Lowell's bastards ruining your looks, Abby. And that's an order.'

Remembering it all now, Abby cringed at the memory. But there had been little she could do. That time, her hands had been tied. She had known instinctively that nothing she said would convince Jake of her reasons for allowing Max to touch her, and time—and experience—had taught her how right she had been.

But, initially, it had seemed a small price to pay. Marriage had not yet become an item between her and Jake, and her reasons for maintaining her independence had seemed convincing enough.

And Max had been amazingly sympathetic, at first. Although he had insisted on her accompanying him on the trip to Bangkok, he had allowed her to return to England without him, and afterwards he had done his best to give her plenty of free time between assignments. Later on, he had even agreed to letting her work for the New York branch of the agency, and as Jake was often in the city she started to live at his apartment.

Of course, Max's motives were not wholly altruistic. He had not been exaggerating when he had said that she was his top model, and that he had no desire to lose her. She brought an incredible amount of advertising to his agency, and her face and figure had become as well known as any celebrity's could be. In addition to which, even he could see that her affair with Jake was adding a new dimension to her visually. She no longer had that untouched, other-worldly innocence, but in its place she had something far more marketable. She had developed the rich, passionate beauty of a woman who knew she was loved, her sensual eyes and parted lips capable of selling anything she was associated with.

For his part, Jake was prepared to be patient. Abby's appealing—if enforced—admission that she would like to go on with her career had been accepted without argument, although she knew Jake didn't really like her being ogled by other men. But during those first few months of their relationship they had so much else going for them, and when they were together nothing else mattered. Even Jake's family—his mother, who resented her, and his sister, who didn't—couldn't spoil their happiness, and when Jake eventually took her to live at his home at Sandbar Abby was ecstatic.

She had heard about his island, of course, and the beautiful house he had built there, but Jake's mother had said it was his private place. He never took any of his women there, she had informed Abby, on that never-to-be-forgotten occasion when she had arrived at the New York apartment and demanded to see her son, so that when Jake took her to live there Abby knew their love was meant to last.

But, she acknowledged now, that was when other things had begun to go wrong. Although Jake put an executive jet at her disposal, it wasn't quite so convenient to keep her appointments half a continent away. Besides which, Jake took to spending more and more time at Sandbar, delegating his responsibilities freely, and expecting her to do the same.

And she wanted to. When they were together, she never wanted them to be apart, and it got harder and harder to leave the island when she knew Jake was waiting there for her.

And, at around the same time, Jake suggested it might be a good idea if they got married. His mother would accept the situation far more rationally if they were man and wife, and in any case he wanted to marry her. He wanted everyone to know it—and most of all Max.

To begin with, it was easy to evade a definite answer: she couldn't think about it now, she was just leaving for Los Angeles; she needed a little time, to be sure they weren't making a mistake. And, to give him his due, Jake was very tolerant. He allowed her weeks and weeks to make up her mind, but inevitably it was something else that made it up for her.

Looking back on it, she had known exactly when Dominic had been conceived. At the first opportunity, Abby had visited a family-planning clinic. With Max's threats still ringing in her head, she had wanted no other complications to mar their relationship, and from then on she had been extremely careful about birth control. It was something Max himself had taught her, and, although the idea of having Jake's baby one day was a heartfelt anticipation, so long as Max held all the cards there was not much she could do.

But, spending so much time at Sandbar, it was far more difficult to remember why she had to be so vigilant. Living with Jake as she was, she began to wonder why she had allowed Max to put her into such a position, and to contemplate Jake's reactions should she tell him the truth. Surely after all this time he could find it in his heart to forgive her for the deception? They meant so much to one another; could such a revelation tear their lives apart? She was to find out sooner than she had thought. And she could pin-point exactly the night Jake had made her pregnant . . .

She had been on a trip to Dallas, in Texas, and, although she had left Jake in New York, during the ten days she was absent he had finished there and flown back to the island. In consequence, Jake's pilot had flown her

in to Laguna Cay at sunset, and as she had walked from
the airstrip to the house, with one of Melinda's grandsons
carrying her bags, she had seen Jake down at the
shoreline.

It had been marvellous to see him again, and, telling
the boy to take her belongings to the house, Abby had
kicked off her shoes and run to meet him. And, in the
breathless urgency of their need for one another, they
had made love there, on the sand, with the scuttling crabs
and screaming gulls for company. Abby hadn't known
if anyone else had seen them, and she hadn't cared. Her
delight in being with Jake again had been the only thing
that mattered, and later, when he'd picked her up in his
arms and carried her into the house to make love to her
again, the idea of scrabbling about in her handbag to
take her pill had been very far from her thoughts.

Of course, she had regretted it later. It was one thing
to fantasise about telling Jake the truth about her and
Max, and quite another to face the actual prospect. How
would he react? She really didn't know. Dared she risk
the chance that Max might have mellowed over the
months and say nothing? Or would he still be as determined to destroy what she and Jake had?

It was a harrowing time, and when she eventually
found out that she was going to have a baby it was almost
a relief. At least now she knew what she had to do. There
was no way she was going to abort Jake's baby. She
wanted it too much.

As luck would have it, she was in London when she
learned, officially, that she was pregnant. Six weeks since
that fateful night at Sandbar, without her period, and
experiencing a distinctly queasy feeling in the mornings,
Abby chose to visit the doctor she used to attend when
she lived in London. But she knew it was just a for-
mality. She already knew how she was feeling. And,
although the idea of facing Max was daunting, somehow

knowing she was carrying Jake's baby had given her more strength.

'Don't tell me. You're pregnant,' Max declared, before she had had the chance to close his office door. 'What a silly little fool you are! I can't believe you did this deliberately—*to me*!'

'I'm sorry, Max,' she said, not knowing how else to answer him. 'But I love Jake, and he loves me. I—I want this baby. I do. I'm sorry if it's inconvenient, but it has been almost two years.'

'Two years.' Max spoke almost reminiscently, and remembering how furious she had expected him to be, Abby was puzzled. This wasn't the reaction she had expected, and she didn't know why but she was scared.

'So,' he went on after a moment, resting his elbows on his desk, and steepling his fingers, 'you're prepared to give up all this—resign at the peak of your success— just to have a *baby*!' He said the word with more force than he had used thus far, and she started. 'As I said before, you're a fool, Abby.'

'It—it's what I want,' she declared swiftly. 'Don't spoil it for me, Max, please.'

'Me? Spoil it for you?' His lips twisted bitterly. 'Oh, Abby, you expect too much.'

'Why do I?' She gazed at him helplessly. 'Max, I've done what you wanted. I've become what you wanted me to be. I've worked hard these last six years to make you proud of me, and you can't deny I've repaid every penny you ever spent on me. I've helped to make the agency the success it is. Why can't you see that I have to have a little life of my own?'

'And after the baby is born?' he suggested, his eyes intent. 'Will you be coming back to work then? Can we expect some delightful pictures of mother and baby to compensate us for nine months of stagnation?'

'No. I—that is...' Abby's tongue circled her dry lips in consternation. Jake would never condone that kind of publicity for his child, she knew. Or for her, once they were married. And he would expect them to get married now. Now that they were going to be a proper family.

'No?' Max inferred. 'I thought not. Your Mr Lowell isn't that kind of animal, is he? He hasn't been too happy about your continuing with your career either, has he? I can just imagine his reaction if I suggest a cosy picture of you nursing junior!'

'You're disgusting!' Abby couldn't disguise her distaste, and Max's face hardened.

'Am I?' he grated. 'Am I really?' He sneered. 'Then it's just as well I anticipated this meeting, isn't it? I'd hate to think you got the jump on me, feeling as you do.'

'What do you mean?' Abby stared at him. 'How could you—anticipate *this* meeting?'

'My dear Abby, do you honestly think Carmella couldn't see what was wrong with you? She's had years and years of dealing with girls who got themselves into one kind of trouble or another. She phoned me a week ago, to tell me her suspicions. Why do you think you're in London at the moment? Hadn't you previously expected to be visiting Japan?'

Abby swallowed. It was true. She had been booked to attend a fashion fair in Tokyo, but Carmella, Max's opposite number in New York, had switched locations. Abby had thought nothing about it at the time, welcoming the chance to visit her own doctor privately. But now the reasons behind it were apparent, and she was suddenly apprehensive of what he meant.

'You mean,' she said unsteadily, 'you sent for me.'

'In a manner of speaking.' Max was disturbingly urbane. 'I wanted you out of the way when Lowell received the news of your previous—liaison. I wanted him to have time to think about it, before you could intervene——'

'You bastard!'

Abby launched herself across the room towards him, but although Max was small he was strong. Besides which, she was weak with disappointment, and desperate to redeem herself in the eyes of the only man she cared about.

She flew back to New York that afternoon, but Jake wasn't at the apartment. Raoul informed her that his master had returned to Sandbar that morning, and, desperate to see him, Abby took the evening flight to Nassau. The following morning she hired a high-powered launch to take her to the island. The inter-island ferry was not running that day and, besides, she doubted she could stand the delay. So much depended on her speaking to Jake immediately, and she found herself praying he would give her a chance to explain.

It was late morning when she reached Laguna Cay. But, by now, she was well known on the island, and no obstacles were put in the way of her disembarking. On the contrary, Andy Joseph himself offered to drive her over to Sandbar, and it was barely twelve o'clock when they reached Oleander Bay.

She remembered that morning as if it were yesterday. The warm sun, the breeze, laden with the scents of the flowers, the buzz of insects in the air, the shushing sound of the ocean.

Jake was in his study, and she knew as soon as she saw him that she was too late. When she asked if he had had any communication with the agency, he regarded her with cold, accusing eyes, and she stumbled into speech without asking him what he had heard.

And it had been hard, *so hard*, to try and justify what she had done. There was no justification, she knew that. She had been eager, and ambitious, just as Max had said. She had allowed herself to be used for the basest reasons, and now he was making her pay for it.

She had been unaware of Jake's dawning horror until she had completed her confession. Pacing about the study, she had paid little attention to his expression, half afraid in truth of what she would find there. But what she had never expected was that Jake should have been hearing something he had definitely not heard before, and only when he said, 'You bitch!' in a strangled, agonised voice did she realise that Max had tricked her again.

'You didn't know?' she choked, and he gave a curt shake of his head. 'But, I thought—you seemed so angry with me!'

'Why wouldn't I be angry?' It was with an obvious effort that Jake summoned the energy to answer her demands. 'God, Abby, how was I supposed to feel, learning you'd gone to London to have an abortion?'

And that was how Max had got his revenge, thought Abby now, pressing a hand to her suddenly nauseous stomach. Even thinking about what had happened was emotionally exhausting, and remembering her own fool-ishness brought unwilling tears to her eyes.

There had been no way to retract what had been said. She had condemned herself out of her own mouth, as Max had intended she should, and even convincing Jake that she was still pregnant, that there was no way she could be persuaded to get rid of his child, had made no difference. Their relationship was over. He said he never wanted to set eyes on her again. And later that day she had been escorted off the island, never to return—until now.

But that had not been quite the end of Jake's in-volvement in her life, as she found out to her cost. Even though she denied him the right to contribute anything to her upkeep during the time she was pregnant, once the baby was born Jake's solicitors moved in. Whether Jake and Abby were unmarried or not, they were able to convince a judge that Jake, and not Abby, should have the responsibility of rearing the child. The fact that she had no job at present, that even when she did she would have to pay someone to look after the baby, while Jake could offer a stable marital environment, had been the clinching factor. Dominic, the only part of Jake left to her, had been taken away, and for several months afterwards Abby had believed her life was over.

Of course, it wasn't. But it had taken another vist from Max to pull her to her senses. His feigned sympathy and offer of employment had made her realise she still had something to offer. But not to him. With the greatest of pleasure, she told him what he could do with his job and found herself another agent, Marcia Stephens, and since then she had never looked back.

Until now...

CHAPTER EIGHT

THE next morning, Abby awakened with a curious feeling of lightness. It was as if the previous evening's reminiscences had had a cathartic effect on her senses, and, while she had no real reason to anticipate the future, she could at least dismiss the mistakes of the past.

Not that she had seen Jake again that day. When she had gone down for supper, Rosabelle had informed her that her employer had asked for his evening meal to be served in his room. 'Perhaps he's takin' good advice, and restin',' the friendly black woman had suggested. But Abby rather thought he was avoiding seeing her.

Nevertheless, this morning she was in a mood to put the past behind her. For the moment she was not disposed to think of leaving, and although it might be foolish she was prepared to do anything she could to change Jake's opinion of her.

It was early, and, sliding out of bed, she went out on to her balcony again, as she had done the day before. But although she scanned the beach quite thoroughly there was no sign of Jake walking along the sand, and, acting on an impulse, she decided to go for a swim.

It was years since she had swum in the ocean, preferring for obvious reasons the comparative privacy of hotel pools on her jaunts around the world. Besides, it wasn't always safe to swim from a public beach, and Marcia had always warned her—as if it were necessary!—to avoid any casual pick-ups.

But this morning the idea of swimming from Jake's private beach, of plunging into the warm waters of the south Atlantic, was irresistibly appealing, and, pulling off her nightshirt, she slipped the psychedelic tabard over her head. The briefs of her bikini made her decent, and, after skilfully plaiting her hair into a single short braid, she left the room.

As on the previous morning, she saw no one as she descended the stairs and let herself out on to the veranda. She could hear a low sound which might have been voices, however, and she guessed Rosabelle and the other members of Jake's staff were sharing an early morning cup of coffee before starting the day.

Outside she paused for a while, breathing deeply of the cool, sharp air. It was so deliciously refreshing, and the view was fantastic. There was so much colour and light and beauty, and she tilted her head back in a gesture of obeisance as she sauntered across the courtyard.

The pool glistened invitingly as she descended the steps to its level. But during the night a handful of insects had landed on its surface, and she guessed it would be attended to before anyone wanted to use it.

She had put on rubber-soled boots to come downstairs, but now she slipped them off and dropped them beside one of the loungers. Then, stretching her arms delightedly, she went down on to the beach.

Although it was still early, the sand still retained a little of the heat from the previous day, and her toes curled appreciatively. There was nothing so satisfying as feeling the grains sliding between her toes, and she bent to pick up a handful, then let them trail away through her fingers.

At the water's edge she paused again, gazing out at the jaws of the reef as the water ebbed and flowed around it. It was as good as a drawbridge, she reflected. Even at high tide, there was no way to float a craft across it.

She turned once, and glanced back towards the house, but nothing was stirring. It was barely seven o'clock, after all, she thought. If her body clock hadn't been out of sync, she doubted if she'd have been awake yet.

With a sigh, she peeled off the silk tabard and stood for a moment, allowing the rising sun to touch her breasts. The cooler air caused her nipples to harden instinctively, and she pulled a rueful face. Then, before she could change her mind, she plunged into the water, catching a convulsive breath as the coolness stung her skin.

Even several yards out from the shore, she was still in comparatively shallow water. In consequence, after the initial chill, she began to appreciate how warm the water really was, and to enjoy the unfamiliar sensation of swimming practically nude. Of course, she and Jake had used to do it all the time—but that was then, and this was now.

Not that she was alone, she reflected wryly, dipping under the waves to survey the underwater kingdom she had invaded. The waters of Oleander Bay teemed with wildlife, and dozens of species of fish swam all around her. There were shoals of tiny silver fish that were almost transparent, as well as the multi-coloured angelfish, and aptly named cardinals. Just occasionally, one of the larger species would come to check her out, but mostly they ignored her, accepting her presence with a charming lack of aggression.

The exercise was good for her, and when she swam back to the shore she was pleasantly tired. Trudging out of the shallows, she sank down wearily on to the sand, resting back on her elbows and turning her face to the sun. She would just rest for a few minutes, she thought, and felt her eyelids drooping.

The slither of silk falling on her skin awakened her, and she blinked her eyes protestingly as someone came to stand over her. The shadow they cast was both a relief and an annoyance: a relief from the sun attacking her bare skin, and an annoyance because she couldn't see who it was.

'I suggest you cover yourself,' remarked a familiar voice, but without the note of censure she had expected to hear. 'I thought you had more sense. You're going to feel pretty sore later.'

Groaning, Abby hauled herself into a sitting position, and the silk tabard, which Jake had dropped over her, fell to her waist. 'What time is it?' she asked, shading her eyes with one hand as she looked up at him, and his eyes narrowed appraisingly.

But it was not Jake who answered her. 'It's nine o'clock!' exclaimed Dominic, from his position opposite his father, and Abby's head swung round in alarm. Clutching the tabard to her breasts, she scrambled to her feet in some embarrassment. Jake might have told her he was not alone, she thought frustratedly.

'We wondered where you were,' Jake added drily, and if he was amused by her appearance he hid it well. 'How long have you been out here? Don't you know you should always tell someone if you're going swimming?'

Abby managed to fumble the tabard over her head, and pulled her braid free of the neckline. Her hair was still wet and encrusted with sand. Much like the rest of her, she thought irritably. She didn't feel half as good now as she'd done when she came out of the water.

'Does it matter?' she muttered in an undertone, and Jake regarded her steadily.

'It matters,' he conceded, using his finger to flick a speck of sand from her cheek. 'And I meant what I said about feeling sore later, too. You've been exposing skin that isn't used to being exposed.'

'My breasts, you mean,' she retorted, gaining a little more confidence as her brain began to function again. She recoiled from his hand. 'Is that what you mean?'

'Something like that,' agreed Jake, without any of his usual hostility. His eyes dropped to the sensuous crests that swelled against the thin silk. 'I've got some cream you might like to borrow. Remind me later, and I'll hunt it out.'

'Where's the rest of your swimsuit?' Dominic demanded now, tugging at her hand, clearly impatient that he was being ignored. 'Have you lost it? Did it come off in the water?'

Abby couldn't prevent the faint tinge of colour that entered her cheeks at her son's words, and it didn't help to have Jake watching her now with unconcealed amusement. 'No—I—I forgot to put it on,' she lied, refusing to look at either of them. 'Um—well, if you'll excuse me I'll go and take a shower. I feel—hot, and sticky.'

'Can I come with you?'

Dominic pulled on her hand again, but this time Jake intervened. 'We'll see Mummy in a little while, after she's had her shower,' he declared smoothly. 'Come on, I've got something I want to show you. Say goodbye to your mother, and we'll see her back at the house.'

Abby took the image of Jake and their son walking hand in hand along the beach back to the house with her. A tall dark man in frayed denim shorts and trainers, and a small dark boy, similarly attired.

She examined her breasts after her shower, but to her relief they didn't appear to have suffered any damage. They were very warm, but that was only natural in the circumstances, and she felt sure Jake had exaggerated just to make her feel bad.

Downstairs again, this time wearing a modest hip-length tunic and Bermudas, she found breakfast waiting for her on the veranda. Orange juice, coffee and a plate of Rosabelle's famous pancakes couldn't be ignored, and, finding she was hungry, Abby said a temporary goodbye to her diet. But it was good to feel relaxed and lazy, and she was still sitting at the table, sipping her fourth cup of coffee, when Jake and Dominic came back from their walk.

Studying the man she had lived with for almost two years, Abby couldn't help thinking that he looked a little better than he had done when she had first arrived. He was still far too thin, of course, but a little of the strain had left his face, and if she didn't know better she would have said he was not displeased to see her there.

'Mummy, Mummy, look!'

As soon as her son saw her, he left his father to dart towards her, clambering on to her knee to show her the enormous conch shell he had brought up from the beach. But over Dominic's head Jake's expression was indulgent, and, pulling out one of the chairs from the table, he straddled it to face her.

'May I?' he asked, lifting the lid of the coffee-pot to discover it was still a quarter full. Then, borrowing her cup, he filled it and raised it to his lips.

'You should have come with us,' said Dominic, distracting Abby from the amazing sight of seeing Jake drinking from her cup, and she forced herself to pay attention to him. 'There were heaps of shells,' he added. 'But none as pretty as this.' He hesitated a moment, and then held it out to her. 'Would you like it? You can have it, if you like.'

'Oh, no, I . . .' Abby shook her head protestingly, her eyes seeking Jake's now in an effort to gain some support. 'Darling, it's your shell. You found it. I couldn't possibly take it from you——'

'He wants you to have it,' Jake inserted flatly, finishing his coffee and putting the cup down. 'If you're refusing because you think I'll mind, don't. It's yours. Be grateful.'

'Well, I am, of course, but . . .' Abby shifted a little awkwardly on her seat, and Dominic wriggled down to the ground.

'Daddy said you could have it,' he declared, causing Jake to look away now. 'He said the colour reminded him of your skin. Don't you think it's pretty? I do.'

Abby's palms were damp as she put the pink-tinged conch shell on the table. 'That was—nice of Daddy, wasn't it?' she murmured, aware of Jake's discomfort now, and loving it. 'Very well, then. Thank you—both— very much. I've never had a nicer gift.'

Jake swung the chair out from under him then, and stood up. 'Well,' he said, raking back his hair with a careless hand, 'if you'll excuse me, I've got some work to do. Be a good boy, Dominic. I'll see you at lunch.'

Abby rose then, stepping into Jake's path as he would have gone into the house. 'Must you?' she said, putting a detaining hand on his arm and feeling the coarse hairs prickling against her skin. 'Why don't you take a day off, for once? It's what you're supposed to be doing.'

But Jake removed her hand with ungentle fingers. 'I don't need you to tell me what I'm supposed to be doing,' he retorted, and now the eyes that met hers were cool and unfriendly. 'Don't go getting the wrong idea, Abby. I still don't want you here. And, if you want me to allow you to stay, I suggest you keep your nose out of my affairs.'

He left them then, but it took Abby several minutes to recover from the coldness of his parting shot. Just when she'd thought they were making some headway, he turned around and treated her like dirt. Which was obviously what he thought about her, she acknowledged, even if she still inflamed his senses.

Still, in spite of Jake's attitude, it was not a bad day, all things considered. It was another day for her to spend with her son, and it was heartening to know that, so far as Dominic was concerned, she could do no wrong.

They played by the pool again in the morning, and then joined Jake for lunch in the shadow of the colonnade. Although Dominic had been into the pool, Abby had not, and there was an awkward silence while Sara took the boy to be cleaned up before the meal. Jake seemed indisposed to talk, and Abby was still brooding over the way he had spoken to her earlier, so they didn't communicate. But when Dominic came back they both made an effort to behave naturally, and only when the boy went for his nap was the status quo resumed.

Deciding she was disinclined to try and humour Jake at present, Abby went up to her room, aware of a slight headache probing at her temple. Maybe she should have a rest too, she thought, flopping down disconsolately on to the bed. Maybe after a sleep she could recover the feeling of anticipation she had felt that morning.

But it didn't happen. She awakened in the late afternoon with a dry mouth, a thumping headache, and a distinctly shivery sense of chill. Not even a warm sweater could erase the coldness that seemed to be emanating from some place inside her, and when she wrapped the woollen cardigan around her she winced at the tenderness of her breasts.

'Oh, no,' she thought disbelievingly, pulling up her tunic to display her burning flesh. She had deliberately not put on a bra since this morning's foolishness to avoid any unnecessary chafing, but now her breasts were red and throbbing with heat, and she hardly dared to touch them.

Jake had been so right, she thought frustratedly, easing the tunic down again and pressing her hands together. She had obviously overdone the exposure, and she wasn't going to escape as easily as she had done the day before.

But the idea of asking Jake for anything, in his present mood, was not appealing. Besides, she was sure that Rosa or her mother would be able to recommend something equally as therapeutic as the ointment Jake had mentioned. So, picking up the phone beside the bed, she pressed the button for the kitchen.

Rosa herself answered her call, and she sounded most concerned when Abby explained, not without some embarrassment, what had happened. 'I'll see what I can do,' she promised. 'You stay where you are, Miz Abby.

I'll get young Sara to tend to Dominic. You just take it easy.'

Abby was content to do just that. She felt distinctly unwell, and, kicking off her shoes, she stretched out on the bed again, one arm raised to block the light from her eyes.

When the knock came at her door, she didn't stir. 'Come in,' she called, wincing as the effort caused a sharp pain to stab at her eyes, and, when the door opened and someone crossed the floor to stand beside the bed, she added weakly, 'Sorry to be such a nuisance, Rosa. Will you just tell Mr Jake, if he asks, that I've got a headache?'

'Why can't you tell him yourself?' enquired Jake drily, his harsh voice less hostile than it had been earlier in the day. And as Abby's eyes jerked open and she struggled up against the pillows, he arched a mocking brow. 'Relax,' he continued calmly, 'I'm not here to argue with you. Rosa says you're sunburned, is that right?'

'As if you didn't know,' retorted Abby painfully, feeling the self-pitying prick of tears at the backs of her eyes. 'And I didn't know Rosa would go running to you with something that I told her in confidence!'

Jake grimaced, tossing the squat jar he was holding between his hands. 'Don't blame Rosa,' he advised her flatly. Then, easing his way down on to the side of the bed, he flicked a hand at her sweater. 'I gather you're in some pain.'

'I can stand it,' said Abby, sniffing resentfully. Then, deciding there was no point in being stupid, she added, 'Is that the ointment? Thank you for bringing it.'

But when she put out her hand to take the jar he held it out of reach. 'Not so fast, Abby,' he averred, as her lips pursed with frustration. 'I suggest you show me the damage. Then I'll be able to ascertain whether you need something more than a herbal remedy——'

'No!' Abby was wide-eyed and indignant, and Jake sighed.

'No, what? No, you don't need anything more than this cream——'

'No, I won't show you!' retorted Abby angrily. 'This isn't a peep show! Just give me the cream, and I'll attend to it myself.'

Jake's face tightened. 'Must I remind you that earlier today you had no such inhibitions about showing me your breasts?' he demanded.

'That's not true.'

'Isn't it? You're not going to pretend that you actually did forget to wear the bra of the bikini, are you? That may have been enough to satisfy Dominic, but——'

'No, I'm not saying that at all,' Abby broke in unsteadily. 'But I didn't intend to fall asleep on the sand, and if I hadn't you wouldn't have seen me.'

Jake's mouth compressed. 'And that's your excuse?'

'It's not an excuse. It's the truth.'

Jake shrugged. 'OK. Have it your way. That doesn't alter the fact that I did see you half-naked this morning, and in your profession I shouldn't have thought nudity was such a big thing.'

'You beast!' Abby caught her breath. 'You know I've never done any nude modelling!'

'Do I?'

'Yes, you do.'

'Well, not for public consumption, I dare say,' he conceded, 'but I guess Cervantes used to be treated to——'

Abby's hand stung as it connected with his cheek, but at least it silenced his ugly accusations. Though, as he reached for her, she did wonder if a verbal assault might not have been better than a physical one.

'You bitch!' he swore angrily, capturing both her hands in one of his and forcing them back over her head. Then, uncaring that he might be hurting her, he dragged the cardigan open and thrust the tunic up above her waist. The bunched material was briefly balked by the fullness of her breasts, but that didn't temper his aggression. Instead, he used brute strength to force the tunic upwards, and Abby sobbed in protest as he cruelly exposed her sensitised skin.

The draught of cool air that touched her body then was at once sharply painful and a relief. It was a relief to escape the bruising rub of her clothes, but even the air abused her flesh. If Jake touched her again, she would scream, she thought, closing her eyes. But when nothing happened she opened them again, to find his face was dark with compassion.

'Lord—I'm sorry,' he muttered, staring at the raw skin. 'Did I do that?'

'Don't be silly.' Abby didn't know what to do. It was humiliating being exposed like this, but to coyly cover her breasts with her hands would have seemed ludicrous. 'It was the sun, wasn't it?' she continued, hoping he would just leave the ointment, which had fallen on the bed during their struggle, and go now. 'You were right. I should have had more sense.'

Jake sighed. 'So why didn't you just tell me what had happened?'

'And have you tell me I told you so?' Abby sniffed. 'No, thanks.'

Jake shook his head. 'I'm not saying that. I *wouldn't* say that. God, left untreated, burns like this can be dangerous.'

Abby glanced down at herself. 'I know.'

'So——' Jake breathed deeply '—I suggest we do something about them.'

'*I'll* do something about them,' corrected Abby tightly, as he found the jar of ointment and began to unscrew the cap. 'Please.' She held out her hand. 'Give it to me.'

'Relax,' retorted Jake, paying no attention to her agitation. Instead, he dipped his fingers into the jar, and they emerged covered in a thick, creamy gel. 'Let me,' he added huskily, and before she could prevent him he began to smooth the ointment over her left breast.

His touch was light, but insistent, his fingers moving slowly and steadily over the tender flesh. And, although Abby resented his arrogant assumption that he had the right to touch her so intimately, she couldn't deny his methods were having some success. Whatever the ointment was, and she suspected she could smell aloes, it was having a most beneficial effect, and the throbbing heat that had burned her skin was definitely subsiding.

'What is that stuff?' she asked, her breath catching in her throat, as he moved to treat her other breast, and Jake lifted heavy-lidded eyes to her.

'I'm not sure,' he confessed shortly. 'But I know it has some analgesic qualities. Why? Does it feel good?'

'Mmm.' Abby's breathing was decidedly uneven now, and she was unwillingly aware that the pain in her breasts was giving way to other, equally unwelcome emotions. It should have been impossible in the circumstances, she thought. Her feelings of anguish and humiliation should have been foremost in her mind. But as Jake continued to stroke her breasts, his touch more a caress than a massage, she felt her body responding in a totally different way.

Her eyes were drawn to Jake's, and what she saw there more than mirrored her own agitation. Jake, too, was becoming aroused by the sensuous movement of his hands, and even as she watched him his thumbs probed gently over her tingling nipples.

'Jake...' she whispered weakly, half in protest, half in submission, but he wasn't listening to her. His whole attention was focused on her mouth, and as she spoke he bent his head and brought his lips to hers.

He was gentle at first, mindful of the pain she had been in earlier, and careful not to cause her any distress. His hands, at either side of her head, kept his weight

from bearing on her, and his lips moved lightly over hers.
But when his tongue circled her lips, and then sought
entry between, Abby felt her control slipping, and, although she knew it was crazy, she let him into her mouth.

The sensual thrust of Jake's invasion was intoxicating, and Abby's hands balled into fists at her sides.
It was the only way she could prevent herself from
winding her arms around his neck, and, although that
was what she wanted to do, she had no intention of rein-
forcing Jake's low opinion of her. It was obvious from
what he had said earlier that he had not forgotten any
part of her relationship with Max, and all she was providing here was a means of assuaging his arousal.

But, for all that, it was heaven to feel his wet tongue
against her teeth. Her lungs and her nose and her mouth
were filled with the taste and the smell of him, and when
he lowered his weight so that his chest was brushing her
breasts her body arched instinctively to narrow the gap
even further.

'Your—your shirt,' she choked, making a last-ditch
attempt to cling on to her senses by warning him that
the cream he had applied earlier would mark the cloth,
but Jake was not alarmed.

'So—it'll stain,' he retorted, fumbling with the fastening without enthusiasm. 'You do it,' he added,
grasping one of her hands and bringing it to his chest.
'Get rid of the buttons. I don't want to hurt you.'

Abby knew she shouldn't do it, but her hands wouldn't
obey the dictates of her brain. Even as she told herself
yet again that Jake would have no respect for her at all
if she let him use her in this way, her fingers were already
tearing the buttons out of their slots. The material parted
easily beneath her hands, and then, groaning his appre-
ciation, Jake closed the space between them.

She wasn't shivering now. At least, not with cold. The
unpleasant after-effects of getting sunburned all seemed
to have gone. Even the soreness of her breasts seemed

to have disappeared, and she moved against him urgently as he crushed her to the bed.

Jake's hands were beneath her now, the tips of his fingers following the nubby contours of her spine, down to the waistband of her shorts. One finger invaded the elasticated waistband, making it easy for the rest of his hand to slide inside, and then his fingers cupped her buttocks, urging her up against him.

His mouth on hers was hungry, hard and passionate, his concern that he shouldn't hurt her disappearing beneath the force of his own needs. His tongue plunged sensuously into her mouth, imitating the possession his body was demanding, and Abby's senses reeled at so many wild sensations.

Jake's arousal was unmistakable, straining the zipper of his tight cotton trousers, as he rubbed himself against her. Whatever else was wrong with him, he was certainly not impotent, she thought unsteadily. Whenever they were together, it was as if a fire consumed them both.

'Still want me to go?' he asked huskily, his breath moistening her ear, and Abby gave up all hope of resisting him. She was actually aching now with the need to feel him hard inside her, and he thrust one leg between hers as if aware of that craving.

Drawing a trembling breath, Abby wound her arms around his neck, dragging her fingers through his hair as she brought his mouth to hers again. If she got pregnant, she got pregnant, she decided recklessly. She wanted Jake; she *needed* him. And just at that moment she didn't much care about the future.

'You didn't answer me,' Jake persisted, his thigh nudging the sensitive juncture of her legs and causing the muscles there to contract around him. 'Do you know what you're doing? This is Jake, remember? Or would Max Cervantes do as well?'

His ugly words penetrated the fog that was clouding her brain. Like an echo of the past, Max's name froze the blood in her veins, and her body jerked convulsively, rejecting the obvious conclusion. Oh, God, she thought sickly, as the implications of what was happening moved into sharp focus. Jake was only doing this to torment her. His arousal might be real enough, but it was obvious he had no intention of satisfying it with her.

With a moan of disbelief, she tried to push him away from her. 'You—you bastard!' she choked, all desire for him evaporating in the aftermath of his provocation. She couldn't wait to get off the bed and put as much space between them as the room would allow. She had been fooling herself. Jake had no intention of either forgiving or forgetting the past.

Surprisingly, or perhaps not so surprisingly in the circumstances, she reflected bitterly, Jake made no attempt to prevent her from dragging herself out from under him. On the contrary, he made it easier, by levering himself back on to his heels and unhurriedly fastening the buttons of his shirt. Abby scrambled off the bed, and, keeping her back to him, peeled the tunic back down over her breasts. Then, when she was sure that no part of her anatomy was exposed to his view, she cast an unwilling glance over her shoulder.

He was tucking his shirt back into his trousers now, but under her contemptuous appraisal he slid off the bed at the opposite side and lifted one mocking eyebrow. 'I thought so,' he remarked, answering his own question, and, ignoring her horrified expression, he sauntered towards the door.

'Get—get out of here!' Abby's voice was high, and on the edge of hysteria, but Jake didn't appear to suffer any remorse.

'I'll tell Rosa you won't be coming down for supper, shall I?' he taunted. 'What shall I say?' He paused. 'How about if I tell her you've got a certain—itch, hmm? An uncontrollable fever that's burning you up!'

Her shoe hit the door as he closed it, and she sank down despairingly on to the bed, burying her hot face in her hands. A fever? she thought tearfully. Yes, that was what she had. A malevolent weakness that wouldn't let go. She shouldn't have come here. Even her love for Dominic was not worth this destruction of her soul. She should have known that seeing Jake again would be disastrous. She simply wasn't the kind of girl to play with her emotions without getting hurt. In spite of everything, she still loved him, and because of that he could destroy her any time he wanted.

CHAPTER NINE

MARCIA phoned the following morning.

Abby was sitting by the pool, safely shaded from the sun by a huge striped umbrella, watching Dominic as he splashed about in the water, when Sara came down the steps from the house carrying a portable receiver.

'Call for you, from England, Miz Stuart,' the black girl declared, holding out the receiver. Unlike the other servants, she never called Dominic's mother Miz Abby. It was as if she wanted to emphasise the fact that she had no right to be here, thought Abby ruefully, taking the phone from her. It was obvious Sara didn't like her. Sara considered her an interloper, and resented the fact that her position, as Dominic's nursemaid, had been usurped.

'Thank you,' Abby said now, as Dominic came to rest his arms along the pool's edge and looked expectantly up at her. 'Oh—Marcia! What a surprise!'

'Who's Marcia?' demanded Dominic, uncaring of the fact that it was a long-distance call. 'Do I know her? Is she that lady who tells you what to do?'

'You could put it like that,' murmured Abby drily, and then, to Marcia, 'Oh—sorry. Dominic was just asking who was calling.'

'If you'd like to take the call indoors, I can stay here with the little one,' said Sara, reminding her that she was still present too, and Abby sighed.

'Well—if you could,' she conceded, realising it was going to be difficult to say anything to Marcia with Dominic listening to every word. 'Um—hold on a second, Marcia. I'm just going into the house.'

148

'I'll come with you.'

Dominic was already starting to scramble out of the pool, but Abby put out a detaining hand. 'No,' she said, ignoring his disappointed expression with an effort. 'Er—you stay here with Sara. I'm just going to tell Marcia what's going on. I won't be more than a few minutes.'

Without giving her son time to initiate another argument, Abby got up from her chair and walked swiftly up the steps and across the courtyard. In actual fact, she would be glad of the chance to speak to someone other than Dominic or one of the servants. Her nerves were badly frayed, and hearing from Marcia was just what she needed.

She took the call in the morning-room, where she and Jake had used to have breakfast when the weather was bad. Sometimes, in September or October, the island could have days of torrential rain, and although it was still hot and humid the winds that accompanied the storms had made sitting outdoors impracticable. Another reason she chose the morning-room was that she could close the door. Many of the reception-rooms opened one from another, and the last thing she wanted was to arouse Jake's curiosity. She hadn't seen him so far this morning, but she knew he would be around, watching her with those mocking eyes, and enjoying her humiliation.

'Abby? Abby, are you still there?'

Marcia's voice dispelled her distraction, and Abby flopped down on to a cushioned rattan chair and put the phone to her ear. 'Yes. Yes, I'm here,' she assured the other woman flatly. 'I'm sorry it took so long, but little pitchers have big ears.'

'Dominic?'

'Dominic,' agreed Abby drily. 'Oh, Marcia, you've no idea how good it is to hear your voice. It seems so long since I left England.'

'Really?' Marcia sounded intrigued. 'Does that mean I'm not going to have a problem in persuading you to

come back to London at the end of the week? That does
surprise me. What's the matter? Isn't it as much fun
playing the good mother as you thought?'

'Oh, no.' Abby sighed. 'I mean—no. That's not it.'

'Dominic's not proving a nuisance, then?'

'Anything but.' Abby was unknowingly defensive. 'As
a matter of fact, Dominic and I are getting along
together really well. It's just that—well, circumstances
aren't exactly as I imagined.'

'What circumstances?'

'We—e—ll,' Abby drew out the word, trying to find
a way to say what she had to say without Marcia's
guessing the whole truth, 'as a matter of fact—Jake's
here. On the island. He isn't in hospital, as I had
anticipated.'

Marcia's confusion was understandable. 'You mean—
he wasn't ill? He didn't collapse?'

'Oh, no. He collapsed all right.' Abby was rueful.
'But—well, Jake being Jake, he discharged himself from
the hospital.'

'Ah.'

'He arrived here the day before I did.' Abby took a
deep breath. 'He wasn't terribly enthusiastic about my
arrival, as you can imagine.'

'I see.' Marcia paused. 'So there's no question of your
bringing Dominic back to England.'

Abby clenched her teeth. 'Not immediately, perhaps.'

'What do you mean?'

'Well...' Abby hesitated. 'I told you Jake's wife had
left him, didn't I? Eve. It seems they're divorced. And
at the moment there's no one, except one of the island
girls, to take care of Dominic.'

'You're not thinking of volunteering for the job, are
you?'

Marcia was momentarily alarmed, but Abby was quick
to reassure her. 'No,' she said. 'No, of course not. I—
I couldn't stay here with Jake. He and I...' Her voice

shook for a moment, and she had to steel herself to continue. 'He and I—well, let's say we cordially—despise one another.'

'So you're coming back to London on Saturday, as arranged.'

'On Saturday?' Abby felt a jolt at the realisation of how little time she had left. Saturday was only two days away. Just two more days to say goodbye to her son.

'Yes, Saturday,' repeated Marcia, her tone a little sharper now. 'That was what we agreed, Abby. One week, that was all. I can't spare you any longer.'

Abby's tongue circled her lips. 'On Saturday,' she said again, her voice distracted. 'But, that means I'd have to leave the island—tomorrow!' Her mind raced. 'The ferry doesn't run on Saturdays.'

'So what?' Marcia snorted. 'A couple of minutes ago, you were saying how long it seemed since you'd left England. I'd have thought you'd be glad to have an excuse for leaving. If you really are serious about you and Jake, that is.'

There was a wealth of innuendo in these last words, and Abby wondered if Marcia had detected the tremor in her voice when she'd spoken of Dominic's father. Leaving the island would mean leaving Jake as well, and, although she knew it was crazy, that idea was tearing her apart.

But now she had to be sensible. Now she had to convince Marcia that she was just as sure of herself today as she had been when she left England. After all, as far as Marcia was concerned, she had come out here to rescue her son, not to get involved with the man who had taken him from her.

'Well?'

Marcia was waiting for an answer, and Abby forced her thoughts away from the memories of last night's lovemaking. Only it hadn't been lovemaking, she told herself fiercely. Jake had only been playing with her. Using her own weakness to degrade her once again.

'Of—course I want to come home,' she got out at last, her fingers tightening convulsively around the receiver. 'It's just that—well, I hadn't actually realised how little time I had left. It's not going to be easy, saying goodbye to Dominic. I—I think he's really beginning to regard me as his mother. It's going to be hard to have to tell him that I've got to leave him again.'

'But you knew that when you went out there,' Marcia reminded her shortly, and Abby sighed.

'Yes. But so long as Jake was in hospital there was always the chance that I might persuade him to let Dominic go.'

Marcia sounded unconvinced. 'It seems to me this sister of Jake's got you out there under false pretences. If the man wouldn't let you keep the child five years ago, I doubt if there's a cat in hell's chance of his changing his mind now.'

Abby quivered. 'I am Dominic's mother!' she exclaimed, stung by the other woman's coldness, and Marcia seemed to realise she had gone too far.

'I know you are,' she said, making a effort to vindicate herself. 'But a man like Jake Lowell doesn't play by our rules.'

'Maybe not.' Abby was forced to acknowledge that she did have a point. 'But when Jake got custody of Dominic, he had a wife. Now that he's divorced, maybe I stand a chance.'

'So what do you propose to do?' Marcia was doing her best to control her impatience, but Abby could hear the edge in her voice. 'Apply for custody through the Bahamian courts?'

'No.' Abby's response was short and resigned. 'I don't know what I'm going to do. I haven't really thought about it.'

Marcia expelled her breath with some relief. 'Well—so I can expect you back in England on Sunday morning, hmm?'

Abby lifted her shoulders for a moment, and then let them fall. 'I—suppose so.'

'Good. I'll phone you Sunday evening then. That will give you time to rest and relax before I tell you of the great new campaign that Guipure want you to launch.'

As Guipure was one of the largest designer perfume houses in the world, the news should have at least raised Abby's spirits, but it didn't. All she could think of was that she had to leave, tomorrow, and imagining how she would feel when she got back to London didn't bear consideration.

It was early in the evening before Abby saw Jake. Although she had spent the day alternately dreading or anticipating his appearance, by late afternoon she was beginning to wonder if he was all right. When he was being nasty to her, it was easy to forget the reasons that had brought her here. She was so busy trying to hide her own feelings, she sometimes lost sight of why Julie had phoned her. But, however much she might despise herself for it, she did still care about him and, no matter what she had told Marcia, she didn't wish him ill.

She was on the point of making some enquiries when she saw Jake walking back from the gymnasium. He was wearing a towelling robe, and trainers, but she doubted he had been using the exercise equipment. In his present condition, that was hardly a sensible equation, and she remembered there were also massage-rooms there, and a Swedish-style sauna, and Jake had once employed a physiotherapist for the convenience of his guests.

Dominic was indoors, having his tea, and Abby had just run upstairs and slipped on one of the cotton summer dresses she had brought with her. It was a pretty thing, patterned with bronze shells on a beige background, and with her becoming trace of tan it gave her skin a creamy glow. Her hair, too, had been bleached a shade lighter by the sun and, caught back from her face in a stumpy pigtail, it exposed the purity of her profile. But as she watched Jake cross the courtyard towards her she was totally unaware of her own attractions. She was going to have to tell him that she was leaving, and that was tying her in knots.

'Looking for me?' he enquired as he neared her, and, instead of going straight into the house as she had expected, he halted by the basin of the fountain and stood for a moment, staring into its depths.

Abby was disconcerted. She had not expected to have to tell him she was leaving quite so precipitately, and, although she had spent the afternoon rehearsing what she was going to say, now that the time had come she felt tongue-tied.

'You had a call today, didn't you?' Jake said unexpectedly, looking at her now with a cool golden gaze. 'I understand it was from your agent. I didn't realise Cervantes had this number. I shall have to get it changed.'

'Max is not my agent, and you know it,' Abby countered, the words springing from her lips instinctively. But then, realising she was being hopelessly predictable, she clamped her jaws together. He knew Max was no longer her agent. With his information network, she was sure there was little about her he didn't know. His only intention had been to annoy her, and once again he had succeeded.

'No,' Jake agreed now, propping his hip on the stone rim of the basin. He folded his arms across his chest. 'No, your agent's name is Marcia Stephens. A rather butch lady, who happens to demand a high standard of moral rectitude in the females she represents.' He paused, his lips twisting. 'I wonder how you managed to convince her of your pre-eminence in that department. It can't have been easy.'

Abby's chest rose and fell with the anger she was suppressing, but she refused to respond to his verbal baiting. In fact, he was doing her a favour, she thought grimly. It was easier to think of leaving when staying involved so much bitterness.

'Well?' Jake prompted, arching his dark brows interrogatively. 'You did have a call, didn't you? Or is that private information?'

Abby took a deep breath. 'I doubt if any call I had here could be regarded as private,' she retorted crisply. 'I wouldn't be surprised if the phone was tapped. That would save you listening at keyholes, or getting the servants to spy on me.'

Jake's mouth twitched. 'Dear me,' he remarked, regarding the faint blush of colour staining her cheeks, 'I must have scraped a nerve. What did Miss Stephens say to you? She must have done something to upset you.'

'Marcia didn't do anything,' Abby responded shortly, and then, realising that once again he was gaining the upper hand, she forced herself to relax. It didn't really matter what he said to her, after all. His opinion of her character was hardly likely to change.

'So it's me,' Jake observed now, surprising her by his honesty. 'I'm the one who's upset you. But it might interest you to know that I haven't been tapping your phone or listening at keyholes. Dominic told me where you were and what you were doing, when I dropped by the pool this morning.'

Abby stared at him. 'You spoke to Dominic this morning?' She shook her head. 'He didn't tell me.'

'Why should he? He and I spending time together is not the rare event you seem to regard it. Believe it or not, I love my son, and I wish I could spend more time with him. I didn't get custody of him just to spite you,

you know. I genuinely believed I could give him a better start in life.'

Abby stiffened. 'You don't expect me to believe that!' she exclaimed. 'My God, if you'd had any thought for anyone but yourself, you'd have left Dominic with me. A child should be with its mother. For the first few *months* of its life, at least!'

Jake looked away from her, his expression thoughtful. 'Yes—well, maybe I was a little—vindictive,' he conceded.

'A *little*?'

'All right, a lot,' he amended tersely. 'You made a fool of me, Abby. No one does that and gets away with it.'

'How did I make a fool of you?' Abby began, and then shook her head. 'No. Don't tell me. I don't want to know.' She made a determined effort to calm herself. 'I—oughtn't you to go and get dressed? You don't want to take a chill, do you?'

Jake got up from the basin, but instead of walking past her and into the house he halted only a few feet away from her. There was a film of sweat on his upper lip now, and she realised he was not as composed as he had appeared from a distance. It reminded her anew that he was still far from well, but she despised the *frisson* of sympathy his appearance aroused.

'Why did she ring?' he asked now, speaking more slowly, obviously fighting to control his breathing. 'Does she want you to go back to London? How long did you tell her you'd be away?'

Abby was tempted not to answer him, but his obvious distress persuaded her to be generous. 'She—I—I have to leave tomorrow,' she admitted reluctantly. 'I only had a week to come here. I start work again on Monday morning.'

A spasm crossed Jake's face at her words, but Abby did not fool herself that she was responsible. Jake was finding it hard to hide his increasing weakness, and even as she thought this he grasped her arm for support.

'Tomorrow's—only—Friday,' he got out, with an evident effort, and Abby turned to look anxiously towards the house.

'I know,' she said, wishing she were not so aware of his muscled thigh brushing her leg. 'But the ferry doesn't run on Saturdays, as you know, and I need to catch Saturday evening's flight.'

'The helicopter—will—take you,' Jake grated harshly, trying to regulate the intakes of air he was gulping. 'I'll—get on—to—Bob Fletcher—tomorrow.'

Abby turned to stare at him. It was the last thing she had anticipated. After last night—and the conversation they had just had—she would have expected him to welcome the precipitation of her departure. She could hardly believe he was actually proposing to prolong the time she had to spend on the island, and, although she was conscious of his tortured breathing, she couldn't prevent her automatic response.

'You mean, you'll actually get Bob Fletcher to fly over from Nassau, on a *Saturday*, just for me?'

'I've—said so—haven't I?' Jake released her arm and took several more uneven breaths. 'But now, you'll have to—excuse me. I think—I need—to rest.'

She would have helped him, but he didn't want it. A grim look in her direction stalled any attempt she might have made to help him inside. Instead, she was left to wonder why he should suddenly have changed his mind about her.

Abby slept badly that night. She should have been relaxed, after gaining a day's reprieve, but her nerves were tense and what sleep she did get was shallow. Jake's kindness had confused her. His willingness to allow her to spend an extra day with her son was not in keeping with his attitude towards her thus far. She was sure there

must be some ulterior motive behind his apparent ben-
evolence, but she couldn't think of one. Nevertheless,
she was still wary of being too trusting.

The following morning Abby had breakfast with
Dominic as usual, and, as she listened to him chattering
on about what they were going to do that day, she wondered how he would react when she told him she was
leaving. It wasn't conceit that made her think he would
miss her when she was gone. In the short time they had
had together, they had got to know one another better
than ever before, and, knowing how alone he had been
before her arrival, she hated the thought of abandoning
him once again. It had been different when he was
younger. Then, she doubted he had really associated her
with being his mother. She had been just another adult—
someone who gave him presents, and treated him with
affection, but who meant no more to him than the
nursemaid who looked after him.

Now, it was different. Now, he was old enough to
understand that he had two parents, and that for some
reason they did not live together. So far, the anomalies
of that situation hadn't occurred to him, but even at five
years of age Dominic had questions that Abby simply
couldn't answer.

They spent the morning on the beach, shunning the
pool in favour of searching for shells. Abby had
explained how, by collecting a lot of different coloured
shells, they could make a picture by sticking the shells
on cardboard, and after having the project demon-
strated to him on the sand Dominic had become quite
enthusiastic. In consequence, the hours before midday
were taken up by beach-combing, and the crabs and other
shellfish they found there made the time simply slip away.

To Abby's surprise, Jake joined them for lunch. As
usual, Dominic and Abby were seated at a glass-topped
table on the veranda, when Jake came strolling out of
the house. Dressed in loose-fitting cotton trousers, and

a sleeveless top, he pulled out the chair beside Dominic and subsided into it, acknowledging Rosa's enquiry as to whether he was going to eat with a careless nod of his head.

He looked pale and weary, as if he hadn't slept terribly well either. There were dark lines around his eyes, and his hair looked as if he had been running his fingers through it pretty extensively. But Abby suspected it was the long-distance phone calls from his office in New York, which kept him closeted in his study most mornings, that were responsible for his haggard appearance. As Melinda had said, he was still far too involved in his corporate affairs to properly adhere to doctor's orders. But Abby had had no success in changing his mind. She was the last person he would listen to.

'So,' he said now, his gaze flickering over Abby before settling on his son. 'What have you been doing this morning? I haven't seen you around the pool.'

'No, we've been c'lecting shells!' Dominic exclaimed eagerly. 'D'you want to see them? They're just over there.'

'After lunch maybe,' said Jake firmly, his warning tone keeping his son in his seat. 'So you've been down on the beach.' His eyes shifted to Abby's. 'I hope you haven't been overdoing it.'

'I've been fully clothed, if that's what you mean,' replied Abby a little stiffly, feeling not much older than her son at that moment. 'Perhaps you should spend more time outdoors,' she added, meeting his gaze with some resentment. 'Then you might not look so pallid.'

Jake's mouth compressed. 'I'm all right.'

'Are you?' Abby was gaining in confidence. 'I got the distinct impression that you were far from all right yesterday evening. And spending all your time in stuffy offices was the reason you ended up in the ICU in the first place.'

Jake cast a meaningful glance in Dominic's direction, but Abby was unperturbed. The boy was happily sucking iced cola through a straw, and not paying any attention to their conversation.

'You're not going to get well if you don't rest,' she continued, giving her attention to the bowl of rice salad in front of her. 'The way you look now, I'd say the prognosis was not favourable. You're working too hard. Let Ray Walker take the strain.'

'It may interest you to know that I haven't been working this morning,' Jake responded suddenly, in a low, intense tone. 'If I look tired, it's because I didn't sleep too well last night. Now, will you get off my case? I didn't let you stay here to give me this much hassle.'

'Why did you let me stay here?' Abby countered huskily, but before Jake could answer Dominic chimed in.

'Me and Mummy are going to make a picture with the shells,' he announced, slurping the last dregs of his cola. 'And then maybe tomorrow we'll make another one. Would you like one, Daddy? To hang in your room.'

Although she was loath to do so, Abby couldn't help looking at Jake then. They both knew she was leaving tomorrow, but Dominic didn't, and this was not the way Abby wanted to tell him.

Jake, however, seemed unperturbed as he answered his son. 'If there's one going spare, I'd be delighted to have it,' he replied, nodding his head towards Dominic's plate. 'Are you going to eat any more of those strawberries? Or have you had enough? If so, I suggest you go and find Sara, and have her put you down for your nap. I want to talk to Mummy.'

Dominic's jaw dropped. 'But you haven't seen the shells,' he protested.

'You can show me later.' Jake smiled as he helped him slide down from his chair. 'Go on, be a good boy. I promise I won't let Mummy beat you to it.'

There was a moment's silence after Dominic had departed. Abby had refused the strawberries, and was presently sipping her second cup of coffee, while Jake, who had started later, was picking at the salad on his plate. For a pregnant spell the only sounds were those of the birds and insects, and the distant thunder of the ocean on the reef.

'You haven't told him you're leaving,' Jake remarked at last, and Abby moved her head in a negative gesture.

'No.'

'Why not?'

'Why do you think?' Abby was defensive. 'I'm not looking forward to leaving him. He's going to think I'm abandoning him, and I'm not.'

Jake pushed his plate aside. 'Don't go, then,' he declared flatly.

Abby caught her breath. 'What did you say?'

Jake looked at her. 'You heard what I said, Abby,' he retorted drily. 'But I'll say it again. Don't go. Stay. At least for another week.'

Abby returned his stare. 'You're asking me to stay?'

'How many more times? Yes. I'm asking you to stay.'

'But—why?'

'For God's sake!' Jake pushed back his chair abruptly, and got to his feet. 'I thought you wanted to stay. I thought you just said you didn't want to abandon Dominic.'

'Well, I don't, of course——'

'There you are, then.'

'But it's not that simple.' She shook her head bewilderedly. 'Jake, I have a job, a career. I can't just abandon my commitments——'

'Oh, no, of course not.' Jake moved to the edge of the veranda, supporting his shoulders against the column that supported the balcony above. 'I'd forgotten, nothing must be allowed to interfere with your ambition. Not loyalty, or integrity; not even the needs of your own son!'

'That's not true!'

'It is true.' Jake's expression was cold as he looked at her now. 'My God, I bet Cervantes didn't even have to cajole you into his bed! You probably jumped at the chance to prove how versatile you were!'

'Don't say that!' Abby jumped up from the table, and faced him on legs that were not quite steady. 'You know it's not true. If I had been as ambitious as you say I am, why am I not still working for Max? Why did I stop working altogether, even after Dominic was born?'

'I don't know, do I?' Jake moved his shoulders in a dismissing gesture. 'I guess Cervantes killed your contract.'

'No.' Abby shook her head. 'No, Max still wanted me to work for the agency, but I wouldn't.'

'Because he'd let your little secret out?'

'No, because he'd blackmailed me into remaining with the agency, long after we—got together.'

'What do you mean?' Jake frowned.

'You asked me to marry you, remember?' Abby drew a steadying breath. 'Why do you really think I refused?'

'Because you wanted to go on with your career——'

'No.' Abby couldn't let him go on thinking that. 'I did it because it was the only way I could keep Max from ruining our lives. But ultimately, he succeeded, didn't he? Albeit with a little help from me.'

Jake stared at her through narrowed eyes. 'You really expect me to believe this?'

'It's the truth.'

'Abby, you were going to abort my child——'

'*No!*' Abby was adamant. 'You know, you can be so stupid sometimes. If I had wanted to have an abortion, why didn't I have one? I could have, couldn't I? I certainly had the opportunity.'

'You didn't do it because somehow you found out that Cervantes had told me what you planned to do,' retorted Jake harshly. 'And as you didn't know exactly what he had told me, you came hot-footing back to Sandbar in the hope of saving the day.'

Abby's shoulders sagged. 'All right.'

'What do you mean—all right?'

'I mean, if that's what you want to believe, I can't stop you.'

'No, you can't.' But Jake's face was pale now, and the familiar flecks of perspiration were appearing on his forehead.

'So—all right.' Abby heaved a sigh. 'But you can't deny that I did leave Max's agency, right at the time when I might have needed him most.'

Jake shrugged. 'So why did you?'

Abby gasped. 'After what he did?'

'As I see it, he only told the truth. Something—something you could have done, any time—any time in the two years we were together.'

'And have you kick me out that much sooner?' she protested scornfully, knowing she shouldn't be arguing with him in his present condition, but unable to prevent the automatic need to defend herself. 'My God, you demand high standards, Jake! Haven't you ever made a mistake?'

'My mistake was getting involved—involved with you,' muttered Jake unevenly. 'As soon—as soon as I saw—who you were with—I—should have—backed off right then.'

Abby blinked. 'But why? What have you got against Max—other than the fact that he wanted me, of course?' Her lips twisted bitterly. 'You should be grateful to him. He saved you from me!'

Jake shook his head. 'You don't—understand . . .'

'Then make me.'

'All right.' But Jake closed his eyes as he spoke, and Abby knew a moment's alarm. Then he opened them again, and looked at her. 'A girl who once worked for me—was invited—by Cervantes—to join his agency. She didn't—she didn't answer an advertisement—as you did. She wasn't that—ambitious. But she was young—and idealistic—and flattered that Cervantes should—consider her—model material.'

Abby caught her breath. The similarity between the story Jake was telling and her own story was remarkable. But, of course, Jake would never believe that now.

'Anyway,' he went on, with an evident effort, 'it didn't work out. Oh—she was a very attractive young woman—but she wasn't—photogenic. My guess is that Cervantes—knew this all along. But—he wanted her—and he was prepared to do anything—anything, to get her.'

'I see.' Abby's voice was cold.

But Jake wasn't finished. 'No, you don't see,' he muttered hoarsely. 'When Cervantes threw her out—she—she killed herself.' He took a strangled breath. 'Somehow—God knows how!—she'd got involved with—with drugs, and she overdosed. The police came to me, because she had no next of kin, and—and I made the arrangements to—to bury her. Now, do you see why I hate Max—Cervantes? And why I despise you, for—for letting him use you?'

Abby groaned. 'He didn't—*use* me.'

'Oh, no. I forgot.' Jake's lips curled contemptuously. 'You used him, didn't you? You'd have done anything to ensure your success.'

CHAPTER TEN

ABBY turned her key in the lock, and let herself into her apartment. Then, closing the door behind her, she leaned back wearily against the panels. She was tired, so tired, she thought dispiritedly. Ever since she had come back to England, she had been fighting a losing battle against the kind of bone-weariness that came from a mental rather than a physical exhaustion, and she was beginning to wonder if she could go on with her work. She no longer had any interest in her career; she attended photographic sessions without willingness or enthusiasm, and if the photographs they took of her did not reflect her state of mind, that was simply good fortune, and not her normal professionalism.

Of course, Marcia was worried about her. She suspected what was wrong, and reacted accordingly. But no heart-to-heart conversations about the foolishness of allowing something that had been over long ago to get to her did any good, and, no matter how convincing Marcia might be, Abby could not put the past behind her.

Perhaps, if she had left Laguna Cay in different circumstances, she would have felt differently. Perhaps, if that conversation with Jake had not taken place, her departure from the island could have been accomplished without any more bitterness. When Jake had invited her to stay on, she should have made a polite refusal and not permitted him to goad her into yet another row. No matter what he said, she did have commitments, and there was no way she could have abdicated her responsi-

bilities, particularly when she had promised Marcia she
would come back.

Even so, leaving the island as she had had not been
the action of a mature woman. Instead of letting Jake
say what he liked to her, and putting up with it for
Dominic's sake, she had chickened out. When she left
Jake on the terrace, she had gone straight to her room
and packed her things. Then, after taking one long,
lingering look at her sleeping son, she had written him
a brief note before tossing her belongings into the back
of the Jeep, and driving away from Sandbar for the last
time.

All the way to the little town of Laguna Cay, she had
prayed that the ferry would not yet have departed. And
she had been lucky, if lucky was finding the ferry still
at the quay. Captain Rodrigues had been more than
willing to take on another passenger, and, if he had
thought her departure was somewhat unprecipitated, he
had been polite enough to keep his thoughts to himself.
No doubt he had imagined that Jake was behind her
hasty flight from the island. And so he had been, Abby
reflected now, although not quite in the way the captain
might have anticipated.

She had wondered if Jake would get in touch with her
once she was back in England, but he hadn't. In the
three months since her return, there had been no word
from either him or Dominic, even though she had written
to her son at least half a dozen times. She hoped someone
had read her letters to Dominic. She was desperately
afraid he might not understand the reasons for her
leaving.

As she straightened away from the door, her feet
nudged the pile of envelopes and circulars that had been
lying on the mat. Bending, she picked up the letters and
scanned through them without interest, and then walked
wearily through to her living-room.

The air in the apartment was warm, and faintly musty. She had been away for the past three days in Scotland, and September in London was proving hotter than anyone had anticipated. Putting the letters aside, she opened the windows to let in some fresh air, letting out a buzzing honey-bee that had been trapped against the panes. Then she sank down on to the chintz-covered sofa and closed her eyes.

She thought at first that the buzz of the security phone meant the bee had returned. She must have lost consciousness for a moment, because when she awakened with a start she felt disorientated, and it took her a few moments to assimilate her surroundings. Then the phone buzzed again, and, realising she had a visitor, Abby got to her feet, almost stumbling over the shoes she had kicked off earlier. She couldn't imagine who it could be. Marcia had been in Scotland with her, but she had gone home to her husband, and at seven o'clock of a Friday evening most people were either preparing a meal or preparing to go out.

Lifting the phone that connected her with the intercom downstairs she tried not to sound impatient. 'Yes?'

'Mummy? Mummy, is that you?'

'Dominic!' Abby could feel her knees buckling, and she groped weakly for a chair to support herself. Was she dreaming? she wondered wildly. Or was she simply hallucinating? It *couldn't* be Dominic downstairs.

'Yes, it's me,' the familiar voice continued into her ear. 'Can we come up? I told Sara you have to press a button to let us in.'

Sara?

Abby blinked disbelievingly, but her finger was already seeking the button he had mentioned, and in a strangled voice she said, 'Please—come on up.'

She was at the door of her apartment when the lift doors opened to expel Sara and Dominic. But no Jake, she noticed, suppressing the pang it gave her. Still, seeing her son again was enough to be going on with. And when he ran into her arms she had to steel herself against the helpless rush of tears.

'I bet you were surprised when you heard my voice,' Dominic declared after a moment, detaching himself from her arms and turning to look at the black girl behind him. 'I told you this was where my mummy lived,' he added proudly. 'Come and see how high we are. You can see all the roofs of the houses, can't you, Mummy? And scrapers, like what Daddy showed me in New York.'

'In a minute, Dominic.' Sara was rather less eager than her small charge, and, although Abby was relieved that her son appeared to harbour no animosity regarding her hasty departure from Laguna Cay, she saw that his nursemaid's eyes were wary. 'Don' you think you should tell your mommy what you're doin' here? She might be goin' out—or entertainin' guests. Anythin'.'

'Oh—yes.'

Dominic looked doubtful now, but Abby couldn't allow that to continue. 'I'm not going out, and I'm not expecting company,' she assured both of them swiftly. 'And I'm very pleased to see you. Um—won't you come in, Sara? We can't talk out here.'

Dominic ran ahead into the apartment as Sara nodded her head before allowing Abby to precede her inside. Then she closed the door behind them and followed Abby into the living-room, stopping inside the door to look about her with interest. Evidently she found the decorations of Abby's apartment to her liking, for her lips formed a perfect 'O' as she gazed about the room.

'It's nice, isn't it?' It was Dominic who spoke first. 'Not as nice as Sandbar, but it's all right.'

His words broke the awkward silence that had fallen, and, with a rueful look in Abby's direction, Sara nodded her head. 'It's very nice,' she agreed, shifting a little awkwardly. It was obvious she didn't feel comfortable here, and Abby was amazed Jake had let her bring Dominic to England.

Still, realising it was up to her to put the other girl at her ease, Abby gestured towards a chair. 'Please,' she said. 'Won't you sit down?' And Sara did so gingerly, perching on the edge of one of the matching chintz-covered armchairs, looking as if at any moment she might make a dash for the door.

Dominic, who had been entranced by the view from the window, now turned to say plaintively, 'Can I have a drink? Daddy promised me a lemonade before we left, but then he was talking on the phone, and I guess he forgot.'

Abby was taken aback. 'You haven't had a drink since you left the island?' she asked disbelievingly. She shook her head, and looked at Sara. 'But—I don't under-stand—how——?'

'Not since we left Laguna Cay!' exclaimed Dominic scornfully, before Sara could make any response. 'Since we left the hotel, of course. Daddy's here in London. Didn't you know?'

Abby swallowed. 'No, I didn't know.'

'Well, he is,' said Dominic airily. 'When he came home from the hospital he said we needed a holiday, and that's why——'

'When he came home from the hospital?' Abby broke in swiftly, her eyes darting from Sara to her son and back again. 'What do you mean, when he came home from the hospital? What hospital? Do you mean before—before I came to Laguna Cay?'

'No,' began Dominic impatiently, but, seeing that Abby was getting agitated, Sara intervened.

'Mr Jake collapsed again, after you came back to England,' she declared in a low voice, twisting her hands together. 'Mr Fletcher took him to the hospital in Miami, and Dominic and me, we stayed with Miz Julie and her husband. But he's better now,' she added, noticing how

Abby had lost what little colour she had as she was speaking. 'Much better. Almost back to normal; don' you think so, Dominic?'

'Can I have a drink?'

Like any five-year-old, Dominic was evidently more concerned with his own creature comforts than with his father's state of health. As far as he was concerned, Jake was invincible, and Abby thought how wonderful it must be to be so irresponsible.

'If you show me where your mommy's kitchen is, I'll get you a drink,' declared Sara, getting abruptly to her feet. She looked at Abby with unexpected sympathy. 'You sit down, Miz—Miz Abby. I'll make you a cup of tea while I'm at it.'

By the time they came back, Abby had herself under control. But the news that Jake had been ill again had been a shock. As much of a shock as learning he was here in London, she thought weakly. She was surprised he had allowed Dominic to come and see her. He must blame her for his second hospitalisation.

The tea Sara had made was strong and sweet, and although Abby never normally took sugar she was grateful for the sustenance it gave her. It was at times like this she wished she had a mother. It would have been wonderful to have someone in whom she could confide.

Sara let Dominic drag her across to the window, while Abby drank her tea, and made suitable noises about the view. She was being so nice, thought Abby ruefully. She wouldn't have expected Sara to be so perceptive.

Then, when Dominic became engrossed in watching a man operating a huge crane on a building site some distance away across the rooftops, Sara came back to her chair. Although she was still not completely sure of herself, it was obvious she was feeling more at ease, and Abby put her cup aside and thanked her for the tea.

'You feelin' better now?' Sara suggested, dismissing any need for gratitude. 'I guess it was a shock, learnin' Mr Jake had been in hospital an' all. But, he wouldn't let Miz Julie tell no one. Mrs Lowell only found out by accident, when she came to visit with her daughter.'

Abby nodded. 'I see.'

Sara hesitated. 'You—you really care about Mr Jake, don' you?' she murmured, barely audibly, and Abby stared at her in surprise. 'You know, I didn' believe it,' she added, her dark face mirroring her remorse. 'Not even when M'linda said so. But you do.'

Abby ran her tongue over her bottom lip. 'Is that why you—resented my being at Sandbar?' she asked softly, and if Sara could have blushed, she would have done so.

'Yes, ma'am.'

'You didn't know why I—why I left the island when I was expecting Dominic?'

'Oh, yes, ma'am. I knew that. But I didn't believe you cared about Mr Jake. Not enough to marry him, and give up your career, leastways.'

Abby shook her head. 'It wasn't quite like that.'

'No, ma'am.' Sara grimaced. 'I see that now. But don' you worry none about Mr Jake. He's all right. How else could he be doin' bus'ness here in London?'

Abby caught her breath. 'He's here on business?'

'Yes, ma'am.'

Abby nodded. 'That sounds like him.'

'Mmm.' Sara nodded too, and then, abruptly, she got to her feet.

'Where are you going?' Abby looked up at her anxiously now, afraid that Sara was about to say they had to be leaving. Was this all Abby was to see of her son? Surely Jake could spare longer than a bare half-hour of his time?

'I'll leave you two alone for a little while,' Sara replied, walking towards the door. But Abby got up too, feeling strangely responsible now that Sara had been so friendly.

'There's no need!' she exclaimed. 'Um—where will you go? Honestly, I don't mind if you stay. I'll make something to eat. We can have it together.'

'That's all right, Miz Abby.' Sara smiled her thanks. 'But Mr Jake's chauffeur is outside, and he'll take me back to the hotel. Mr Jake said to tell you he'd send for the boy later. That is, if you meant what you said about not goin' anywheres.'

'Oh, no. No.' Abby glanced round anxiously at Dominic, and then looked at Sara again. 'Er—thank you. Thank you for bringing him. And—thank you for believing me. I do appreciate it. Honestly.'

Sara smiled again, and then, with a wave to Dominic, she let herself out of the apartment. Abby followed her to the door, turning the key in the lock and attaching the safety chain; then she went back to her son.

An hour later, Abby was thinking how empty the apartment would seem when Dominic had gone. Already the floor was strewn with the toys that she had kept at the apartment for his visits, and, although most of the things were too young for him now, he seemed to enjoy playing with them. There was a half-empty glass of orange juice on the polished surface of the coffee-table, too, and biscuit crumbs littered the carpet. And in the dining-room the remains of the pizza he had chosen from the freezer for his supper was congealing on his plate.

Abby was piling up the building bricks for the umpteenth time when the buzzer sounded, heralding Sara's return. Although her heart turned over at the thought that any minute Dominic was going to be leaving, her son showed no such misgivings as he scrambled to his feet.

'Can I do it? Can I do it?' he demanded, remembering from previous visits how to press the button, and

Abby lifted him so that he could pick up the receiver. 'Yes,' he said, mimicking Abby's response earlier, but she nearly dropped him when a gravelly masculine voice asked,

'Is your mummy there?'

'It's Daddy! It's Daddy!' Dominic exclaimed, stating the obvious, and, setting her protesting son on his feet, Abby took hold of the receiver.

'Jake?'

'Who else?' But he sounded uncertain. 'Can I come up?'

Abby hesitated. Jake had never been in this apartment. She had leased her old apartment when she went to live and work in the States, and then, when she came back, she had sold it, not wanting the memories it evoked. This apartment was hers, and hers alone. No man had ever shared her bed here, or used the bathroom, leaving shaving soap all over the mirror. Did she really want Jake to disrupt its neutrality, when the peace that she had found here had been so hard won?

'Press the button, Mummy.'

Dominic was growing impatient, and Abby looked down at him with troubled eyes. When you were five years old, everything was so simple. Someone knocked at the door, and you opened it. Someone stepped on your heart, and you survived.

'Mummy!' Dominic gazed up at her appealingly. 'Mummy, it's Daddy. Press the button. There it is. There.' He stretched up a small finger and indicated, and then, when she still did nothing about it, he managed to depress it himself.

'Oh, Dominic!' Abby came to life then, but it was too late. Already the security door downstairs would have opened, and, meeting her son's belatedly anxious eyes, she knew she couldn't be cross with him. After all, Jake was his father. And what more natural to him but that she should let him in?

Realising there was no way she could avoid the inevitable without hurting her son, Abby put her own feelings aside and unlocked the door. Then, releasing the chain, she allowed Dominic out into the corridor, hearing the whine of the lift as he skipped towards the gates.

Surprisingly, it was Sara who emerged first from the lift, but Dominic barely paused to give her a smile before grabbing his father's hand. 'I pressed the button to let you in!' he exclaimed proudly, as Jake stepped into the corridor. 'Mummy forgot where it was, but I remembered.'

'Did you?'

Jake seemed to speak with an effort, and for a moment Abby was afraid he was still far from well. But he obviously looked much better—albeit not a lot heavier—and she could tell by the way he moved, and by the clear brilliance of his eyes, that his hesitation had not been purely physical.

'Abby,' he said now, meeting her anxious gaze with a guarded appraisal. 'I hope you don't mind my coming here. I wanted to see you, and it seemed the best way, in the circumstances.'

'What circumstances?'

Now that she could see that Jake was in perfect control of his faculties, Abby felt a kindling sense of resentment. What now? she wondered. What possible reason could he have for coming here?

'The circumstances that warrant my talking with you— privately,' said Jake now, glancing round at the black girl. 'Sara, will you take Dominic back to the hotel, please?' And when Dominic started to protest, 'Do as you're told, son. You'll see your mummy again tomorrow, I promise. But right now we have things to say to one another. Things that a little boy like you wouldn't understand.'

'Do we?' Abby was on the point of arguing with him, but the realisation that both Sara and Dominic would be a party to her objections closed her mouth.

'But I want to sleep here tonight,' Dominic insisted, looking up at his father, and then his mother, with equally indignant eyes. 'You said I could stay with Mummy,' he finally accused Jake, with resentment. 'I don't want to go back to the hotel.'

Abby, whose own eyes had widened at this unexpected announcement, now looked at Jake, too, for an explanation, but he did not seem disposed to give it.

'Tomorrow,' was all he said, impaling his son with a warning look and, although he huffed and puffed a little, Dominic knew the argument was over.

'Say goodnight to your mommy,' Sara advised gently, pushing him forward, and, unable to offer him any further reassurance, Abby gave him a hug. 'I'll see you tomorrow,' she said, unconsciously taking Jake's word for it. 'Be a good boy for Sara, hmm?'

She waited until Sara and Dominic had gone into the lift and the gates had closed before turning back into the apartment. Although she told herself that the anger she had felt earlier was justifiable, she was confused now, and when Jake asked, 'Can I come in?' she gave a helpless shrug of her shoulders.

'Can I stop you?' she countered, preceding him into the apartment, and her nerves tightened when he closed the door and followed her into the living-room.

The room was just as untidy now as it had been before she'd answered the door, but somehow it looked worse. She guessed she was seeing it through Jake's eyes, and she could imagine his reaction to the mess. But she didn't have a staff of servants waiting to pick up after her. Just a twice-weekly cleaner, who was more of a friend than an employee.

'I guess Dominic is responsible for this,' Jake remarked, surveying the room with a wry smile, and Abby made a careless gesture.

'We both are,' she replied shortly, suddenly conscious of her own dishevelled appearance. After Sara had left she had changed out of the elegant linen suit she had worn to travel in, into a pair of baggy cotton trousers and a T-shirt. Ideal wear for playing with a small boy, she had thought; not so ideal for entertaining the small boy's father.

Jake shrugged now, and glanced around. 'May I sit down?'

Abby's tongue circled her lower lip. 'If you can find somewhere,' she conceded ungraciously. But Jake, in his glove-fitting suit of pale grey silk, was making her nervous, and she wished he would just state his business and go.

Yet she couldn't deny that she did get a certain pleasure out of just looking at him. His lean face and tautly muscled body were so painfully familiar, and now that he had recovered his strength his dark skin did not have the sallowness it had possessed three months ago. Yet, for all that, there was still a trace of uneasiness in his manner, and if she hadn't known him better she would have said that he was nervous, too.

Not knowing what to do—whether to stand up or sit down, tidy the room, or leave it as it was—Abby pressed her hands together and faced him, as he seated himself on the sofa. She wasn't in the mood for polite conversation, and despite what he had said about Dominic she couldn't believe Jake had any serious reason for being here.

'Why don't you sit down?' he asked now, looking up at her with faint impatience. 'I promise I won't jump on you. Not unless you ask me to, of course.'

Abby subsided into an armchair rather suddenly. 'Is that supposed to be funny?' she countered, not wanting

him to notice how much his words had affected her. 'I—
what are you doing here, Jake? What possible gratifi-
cation can you get from making fun of me?'

'I'm not making fun of you, Abby,' he assured her
flatly. 'Myself, perhaps.' He paused. 'I thought you
might be glad to see Dominic, at least. He was pretty
upset when you walked out on him like that.'

'Of course I'm pleased to see Dominic.' Abby bent
her head. 'And—and I was pretty upset myself when I
left the island.' Taking a deep breath, she forced herself
to look up at him. 'I—I was sorry to hear you had been
ill again. Sara told me you had to go back into hospital.'

'Yes, I did.' Jake loosened the buttons of his jacket,
and stretched his arms along the back of the sofa. The
action strained the buttons of his shirt, exposing glimpses
of the brown flesh beneath. 'I guess it was on the cards
all along. You were right. I needed a complete break
from business. You may be interested to know that, as
of two weeks ago, Ray Walker is effectively running the
corporation.'

'I see.' Abby couldn't hide her surprise. 'But Sara said
you were here on business.'

'Private business,' amended Jake without elabor-
ating. He paused. 'Do you have a drink around here?'

Abby took a deep breath. 'Um—I have some sherry.
That's all.'

Jake grimaced. 'So—am I to be offered one? It wasn't
a rhetorical question. I really could use a drink.'

Abby hesitated a moment, and then got to her feet
and crossed to the door that led into the small dining-
room, and from there into the kitchen. The additional
disorder on the dining-room table warranted only a
passing glance. Once Jake had gone she would be glad
of something to do, she thought unsteadily.

The sherry was in the cupboard over the sink: a half-
empty bottle of a rather indifferent wine that she had
occasionally used for cooking. As she seldom drank al-

cohol herself, and then only wine, she didn't keep spirits
in the apartment.

Still, it would have to do, she decided tensely, opening
another cupboard and finding a glass. It wasn't her fault
if Jake came here unannounced and uninvited. Goodness
knew, she didn't want him here, she thought despairingly. This was her home, and his being here was viol-
ating it.

Because she was allowing herself to get agitated, her
hand shook as she tried to pour the sherry into the glass.
In consequence, a fair portion of it ended up on the
marble worktop, seeping off the edge and dripping on
to the floor tiles.

'Oh—*damn*!' she muttered, half tearfully now, her
emotions definitely getting the better of her, but when
she swung around to get some tissues to blot up the
spillage she slammed into Jake right behind her.

'Hey!' he exclaimed, capturing her flailing hands.
'What's going on?' He looked over her shoulder. 'Oh,
I see. Complications.'

'It's nothing.'

But the words were choked and muffled, and Jake
had never been unperceptive where she was concerned.
Realising she was on the verge of tears, he gave a rueful
grin. 'Look, if you don't want me to have a drink, then
it's OK. I'll survive.'

'It's not that,' said Abby, trying to extricate herself
from him, and scrubbing the knuckles of one hand across
her cheek. 'I—I'm just—tired, that's all. It's been a long
day.'

'Has it?' Jake looked at her intently. 'And I've made
it longer, right?'

Abby shook her head, not trusting herself to speak.
She couldn't cope with him in this mood. It would have
been easier if he had been sarcastic with her. Right now,
his kindness was more than she could take.

'You know, come to think of it, you do look tired,' he conceded now, not making any effort to move out of her way. His thumb smeared away a treacherous tear. 'Am I responsible for this?'

'For my being tired?' Abby spoke in an abnormally high voice, the effort of holding back her emotions causing a consequent rise in her vocal range. 'No, of course not. I've just spent three strenuous days in Scotland. But it's good to know I look as haggard as I feel. Thanks. That really does my ego a power of good——'

'Don't be silly.' Jake's voice had an edge to it now. 'You know perfectly well you could never look haggard! I just meant——'

'I know what you meant.'

'No, damn you, you don't!' Jake retorted harshly, preventing her from forcing her way past him. The kitchen was small, and it wasn't difficult. 'For some reason, you seem determined to think the worst of me!'

'The worst of you!' Abby's voice came back to normal as anger took over from emotion. 'That's my line, surely. It's what you've thought of me long enough, isn't it?' She took a breath. 'Oh, this is ridiculous! I don't want to argue with you, Jake——'

'Don't you?' Jake resisted her efforts to evade him, and, cupping her neck between his palms, he used his thumbs to tilt her face up to his. 'Well, don't look now, but you're making a pretty good job of it.'

'Oh...'

His teasing rejoinder, when she had expected another bitter outburst, was the last straw and, giving in to an uncontrollable impulse, she allowed her head to droop forward until her forehead came into contact with the silky material of his shirt. There was so much comfort in that tenuous connection and beneath his shirt his body was warm and reassuring. His heart was beating steadily and evenly, if a little faster than she had expected, and

just for a moment she allowed herself to absorb a little
of his strength. If only, she thought despairingly, and
then, realising where her thoughts were leading, she made
an effort to draw back from him.

But while she had been savouring the delight of being
close to him again, Jake's arms had encircled her in an
enveloping embrace, and when she tried to step back
from him she was made acutely aware of it. In her involuntary need to touch him, she had invited his partici-
pation, and now the muscles of his chest and abdomen
were pressing against hers, his thigh nudging her legs to
part to promote a greater intimacy.

'Jake . . .' she began unsteadily, her hands gripping his
upper arms in an effort to put some space between them.
But, when she looked up at him, Jake bent his head and
brushed his mouth against hers.

Immediately her body was awash with anticipation.
Even after all that had gone before, when he touched
her her whole body reacted, the blood running wildly
through her veins. And the mindless pleasure his kiss
evoked never failed to excite her.

'Why—why did you come here?' she got out protestingly, when his lips moved to caress the quivering column
of her throat, and Jake groaned.

'Not now.'

'Yes, now,' she averred unsteadily, even though her
shoulder lifted to his sensuous touch, like a flower to
the sun. 'How do I know you're not just—just tormenting me, as you did before?'

'Tormenting myself, more likely,' muttered Jake
against her ear. He grasped one of her hands and pushed
it down between them. 'Does that feel as if I'm tormenting you?' he demanded, as his arousal throbbed
against her palm, hot and hard beneath the cloth of his
trousers. 'God, Abby, I want you! Don't—don't stop
me now.'

Abby knew she ought to stop him. After what had happened that night on the island, she ought to be able to tell him to get lost, to get out of here now, before anything irrevocable happened; but she didn't. She told herself it was because she was tired, that she had no strength left with which to fight him, that he was stronger than she was anyway, and in any contest he would come out the winner, but it was none of those things. When his mouth returned to hers, and his tongue slid sensuously over hers, she lost all will to do anything but respond to his demands. She had been wanting him for so long, and being here, in his arms, felt right, *so right*.

'Let's find somewhere more comfortable,' muttered Jake thickly, dragging his mouth from hers with an effort, and Abby nodded. Holding her hand, he tugged her after him, through the dining-room and living-room again and, with her assistance, into the pink and gold femininity of her bedroom. Then, pulling her down on to the bed beside him, he covered her with his body, and she revelled in the overpowering possession of his muscled frame.

'This is much—much better,' he added unevenly. 'Oh, God, Abby, I was afraid I'd lost you.'

His continued weight was making her breathless, and with a shaky sigh she whispered softly, 'Not yet. But if you don't give me a little air, you might.'

'Oh!' Immediately he rolled to one side, shrugging out of his jacket as he did so, and tossing it on the floor. 'I'm sorry,' he said, burying his face in the hollow between her breasts. 'I just needed to be close to you.'

'Me, too.' Abby wound her arms around his neck. 'Oh, Jake, kiss me...'

He needed no second bidding. His mouth on hers was hot and hungry, and beneath his sensual assault Abby responded wildly. She was in love with this man, she had been in love with him for more than eight years, and nothing, and no one, had been able to alter that situation.

Jake's hands sought her breasts, his mouth whispering his approval when he discovered she was not wearing a bra. The T-shirt was easily disposed of, and beneath his abrasive thumbs her nipples swelled and hardened.

Then he pulled down the cotton trousers, his mouth twisting sensually when he saw the lacy briefs she was wearing. Unable to resist, his hand moved to the apex of her legs and rubbed against the silky cloth. Then his fingers probed beneath the lace to find her moistened core.

He watched her as she arched against his probing fingers, and then drew her hands to his body. 'Undress me,' he said hoarsely as waves of pleasure swept over her, and, pushing herself into a sitting position, she tore open the buttons of his shirt.

He helped her with his trousers, but let her peel his underpants off his legs. His manhood spilled into her hands, and she rubbed herself against him, arousing him to such an extent that he had to pull himself away from her.

'If you don't let me go, this is going to be the shortest lovemaking on record,' he muttered huskily, as her hands lingered around the curls of hair that arrowed down between his legs. He spread her legs and thrust himself into her. 'Oh, God, that's better. I'm sorry but I just can't wait.'

Their climax was simultaneous, and, although Jake had been afraid she would not enjoy it, Abby was equally as aroused as he. Just the feel of Jake's hard body possessing her, stretching her, filling her, drove her almost to the brink of insanity, and the harmony of their bodies created a perfect act of union. Abby felt exhilarated, sated, lost in a world of mindless ecstasy that only Jake had ever been able to achieve. She wanted to wind herself around him, get inside him if she could, keep him close beside her, for however long they lived.

It was some minutes before she felt Jake nuzzling her jaw, his teeth catching teasingly at her lower lip, and tugging insistently. 'It was good,' he said, his words both a statement and a question, and Abby gave a lazy, sleepy sigh.

'It was good,' she echoed, her hands sliding possess-ively into his hair. His forehead was slightly damp, as hers was, but his hair was thick and virile, clinging to her fingers.

'And you are happy?' he persisted, shifting slightly so that he could look down into her face.

'Hmm. Happy,' she agreed, allowing her fingers to trail along his jaw.

'So—why these?' he murmured, bending to brush her skin with his tongue. 'Salty,' he said, savouring the taste of her, and Abby's hand came up to discover there were tears moistening her cheek.

'Oh, *damn*!' she exclaimed, sniffing and scrubbing the tears away. But it was as if, subconsciously, she had known how reckless she was being. That making love was not the same as loving, and Jake had not said he loved her. He had said he wanted her, and he had. She had no doubts about that. But how much did he want her? And for how long?

Taking advantage of his relaxed state, she managed to roll away from him, sliding off the bed and grabbing her bathrobe from the back of the door. Then, tying the belt tightly around her, she turned to face him, her eyes bright with unshed tears, her throat tight with emotion.

'I—I think I need a glass of that sherry now,' she averred, trying to speak lightly. 'Shall we—shall we have it in the other room? It won't take long to tidy up.'

'Forget the other room, and the sherry,' declared Jake flatly, levering himself up with some reluctance and gazing at her steadily. 'What's going on, Abby? Why are you crying? My God—I thought we understood one another. Don't tell me this was all a mistake.'

Abby sniffed again, bending her head to examine the folds of the bathrobe in an effort to regain her composure. But seeing him, sitting there, blatant in his masculinity, was tearing her apart. She would never sleep in that bed again, she thought, without remembering how it had been.

'Abby!' His voice was gentler now, as if sensing the precarious state of her nerves, and she drew a trembling breath. 'Abby, what happened just now—you wanted it as much as I, didn't you? God, I know you did. I may be arrogant, but I'm not feeble-minded.'

'All right.' Abby forced herself to look up at him. 'All right. Yes. I wanted you to make love to me. But I still don't know why you wanted to, do I? When I was at Sandbar——'

'When you were at Sandbar, I was a fool,' said Jake harshly. 'I wanted you then, but I was too proud to admit it. And then—when you'd gone—it was too late.'

Abby's breathing was shallow. 'I'm sorry,' she said in a small voice, not really believing what he was saying, and Jake gave a mirthless laugh.

'You're sorry,' he said unsteadily. 'Why should you be sorry? Because of me, we've wasted six years of our lives. I'm the one who's sorry. Sorry I ever listened to Cervantes' filthy lies!'

Abby blinked. 'You mean—you mean Max did tell you about—about me?'

Jake sighed. 'Not half soon enough.'

'What do you mean?' Abby was confused.

Jake looked at her with heavy-lidded eyes. 'Do you remember the day you left the island? Not six years ago. Three months ago?'

'Yes.'

'That was the day I spoke to Cervantes.'

Abby shook her head. 'But—why?'

Jake took a moment to consider his words, and then he said quietly, 'Do you remember what we spoke about, the day you left?'

Abby frowned. 'Not—not exactly.'

'You don't remember telling me that he had black-mailed you into remaining with his agency after you and I got together?'

Abby hunched her shoulders. 'Oh—that.'

'Yes, that,' said Jake evenly. 'I'm not proud of what I did, but I was desperate to prove you wrong.'

'I see.'

'No, you don't see.' Jake stared at her imploringly. 'Abby, for six years I'd been trying to forget you. And I couldn't. When I saw you that first afternoon at Sandbar, I guessed I'd just been wasting my time, but I wouldn't accept it. I know now that love like ours—love such as I felt, and still feel for you doesn't just die to order. Oh, it wilts a little, particularly if it's left to wither, but it only needs the slightest encouragement to flourish once again.'

'Jake——'

'No. Listen to me. That was why I wanted to speak to Cervantes. It was my last chance to prove to myself that I hadn't made a mistake.'

'But what did you say to Max?'

'*Max!*' Jake said the man's name with loathing. 'Sometimes I think I should kill him. Goodness knows, I've thought about it often enough. These past three months, particularly when I was in the hospital, I used to fantasise about the way I would do it. But now that I'm well again, and able to choke the life out of him, I find the idea of trading my freedom for his life just isn't worth the candle.'

'Oh, Jake!' Abby came to wrap her fingers around the brass rail at the foot of the bed, and Jake moved so that his thigh was touching her fingers.

'I love you, Abby,' he said simply, his hand running possessively along her jawline. 'And I want to make love to you again, very badly. But I can't until I've told you everything.'

Abby nodded. 'So go on.'

Jake took a deep breath. 'OK. I guess I got to speak to Cervantes about the same time the ferry was leaving Laguna Cay. The time change and all meant it was evening when I reached him. He was at home, for which I'm eternally grateful. I'd hate to think our conversation ended up on his tape.'

Abby bit her lip. 'What did he say?'

'Eventually, everything,' said Jake flatly. 'Oh, at first he simply endorsed what you had said, with embellishments. He maintained that you had known the score, right from the beginning, and that you and he had been lovers for two years when I met you.'

'Oh, God!' Abby felt sick. Would Max's lies never end?

'But that was his mistake,' said Jake softly, as she closed her eyes against the images his words had evoked. 'Like a bolt from the blue, I remembered the first time I made love to you. And there was no way you could have faked what happened. You were innocent, Abby. I knew it at the time, and I knew it then. Only, somewhere in between, I'd allowed the memory to slip.' He groaned. 'If only I hadn't been such a blind fool six years ago! If only I'd used my brain then, instead of letting my emotions rule my head!'

Abby trembled. 'Do you mean it?'

'Do you doubt it?' he demanded huskily, drawing her towards him and allowing his tongue to stroke her quivering lips. 'Oh, Abby! Can you ever forgive me?'

Abby spent the next few minutes proving that she could, but later, when she was flushed and contented, naked once more against the pillows, she asked gently, 'But—how did you get Max to tell you the truth?'

Jake sighed. But then, realising she deserved to know everything, he nodded. 'Do you remember that story I told you, about the girl who took the overdose?' Abby nodded. 'Well, I threatened him with exposure to the media. Oh, I doubt if I could have made the story stick, and it would probably have cost me a small fortune in damages, but mud clings, as we both know, and he knew that that kind of publicity wouldn't enhance his agency's reputation.'

'Oh, Jake.' Abby wound her arms around his neck, and pulled him down to her. 'I love you.'

'I know.' He buried his face in the scented hollow at her nape. 'Just go on telling me, and I'll believe it's true.'

Abby stroked his shoulder. 'You really are well again, now, aren't you?' she ventured anxiously. 'I was so worried when Sara told me what had happened. It was all my fault.'

'No. It was my fault, and Cervantes'.' asserted Jake firmly. 'And Sara told me how you felt. How else do you think I found the courage to come round here this evening?'

Abby frowned. 'But—you did intend to see me, didn't you?'

'Are you kidding?' Jake nuzzled her breast. 'My darling, you're the only reason Ray Walker is running the company, and I'm here in London. As soon as I was able to travel, this was my destination.'

Abby made a sound of contentment. 'Dominic's going to be so pleased.'

'Especially when his parents decide to tie the knot at last,' agreed Jake drily. 'You will marry me, won't you? You can go on with your career. I promise I won't make any demands on you that you don't feel able to fulfil.'

Abby's fingers tangled in his hair, pulling his face up so that she could look at him. 'What career?' she asked huskily. 'You're my career. And Dominic. And any other children we might have. Marcia will understand. She knows my heart hasn't been in it ever since I got back from the island.'

Jake's mouth seared hers. 'I hoped you'd say that. But—I mean what I say. If you ever get bored——'

'With you?' Abby wound one slender leg around his thigh. 'I can't imagine anything less likely. I'm going to be much too busy to be bored. Don't you agree?'

And he did.

Zodiac Wordsearch
Competition

How would you like a years supply of Mills & Boon Romances ABSOLUTELY FREE?

Well, you can win them! All you have to do is complete the word puzzle below and send it into us by Dec 31st 1990. The first five correct entries picked out of the bag after this date will each win a years supply of Mills & Boon Romances (Six books every month - worth over £100!) What could be easier?

S	E	C	S	I	P	R	I	A	M	F
I	U	L	C	A	N	C	E	R	L	I
S	A	I	N	I	M	E	G	N	S	R
C	A	P	R	I	C	O	R	N	U	E
S	E	I	R	A	N	G	I	S	I	O
Z	O	D	W	A	T	E	R	B	R	I
O	G	A	H	M	A	T	O	O	O	A
D	R	R	T	O	U	N	I	R	U	R
I	I	B	R	O	R	O	M	G	Q	O
A	V	I	A	N	U	A	N	C	A	C
C	E	L	E	O	S	T	A	R	S	S

Pisces	Aries	Leo	Earth
Cancer	Gemini	Virgo	Star
Scorpio	Taurus	Fire	Sign
Aquarius	Libra	Water	Moon
Capricorn	Sagittarius	Zodiac	Air

Please turn over for entry details

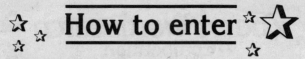

How to enter

All the words listed overleaf, below the word puzzle, are hidden in the grid. You can can find them by reading the letters forwards, backwards, up and down, or diagonally. When you find a word, circle it, or put a line through it. After you have found all the words, the left-over letters will spell a secret message that you can read from left to right, from the top of the puzzle through to the bottom.

Don't forget to fill in your name and address in the space provided and pop this page in an envelope (you don't need a stamp) and post it today. Competition closes Dec 31st 1990.

Only one entry per household (more than one will render the entry invalid).

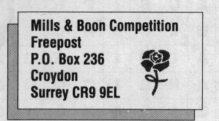

Mills & Boon Competition
Freepost
P.O. Box 236
Croydon
Surrey CR9 9EL

Hidden message _____

_____

Are you a Reader Service subscriber.   Yes ☐   No ☐

Name_____

Address_____

_____

_____

_____ **Postcode**_____